Ex Libris

BOMBUS
BOOKS

# Imagine Oxford

Edited by Jackie Vickers

An environmentally friendly book printed and bound in England by
www.printondemand-worldwide.com

This book is made entirely of chain-of-custody materials

BOMBUS BOOKS

15 Henleys Lane, Drayton, OX14 4HU

www.bombusbooks.co.uk

www.fast-print.net/store.php

Imagine Oxford

ISBN 978-178035-371-5

First published 2012 by
BOMBUS BOOKS
An imprint of Fast-Print Publishing
Peterborough, England.

# *Contents*

# *Introduction*

Ａll these stories have appeared in previous Oxford collections which, although successful, became prematurely out of print. Demand for them continues, however, so those of the original authors who are members of the Oxford Inc. writing group have decided to reissue their contributions in this new book. In doing so they would like to acknowledge the inspiration, enthusiasm and encouragement of novelist and teacher Sara Banerji, without which few of these stories would have been written.

Although all of them have a basis in reality, they take the reader into an imagined Oxford in which, for example, an old portrait seems to smile at an American tourist, a summer's punting has unexpected consequences and gargoyles come to life. More prosaically, there are problems in a tattoo studio and with parking in the Westgate multi-story. Each one concludes with some background on the real-life people, places and events on which it is based.

Oxford is a magical place as every resident knows and as visitors soon discover. It has inspired scholars and writers for centuries and spawned politicians, scientists and a good few eccentrics. As this entertaining collection shows, every corner is bursting with humour, mystery and romance.

Jackie Vickers

May 2012

# An Alice Story

## *Andrew Bax*

C an you feel a shadow pass? Can you hear it? Of course not, Alice said to herself as she trampled down some nettles to get at the next grave. But something like that had just flickered by. This was the middle of Oxford; she could hear the city's bustle not far away. It must have been a bird.

She studied the flowery exuberance of Victorian masonry, and picking away some lichen from the deeply-pitted inscription, she read, 'Taken Away in the Service of Her Majesty's Glorious Empire in India . . .' Not what she was looking for. Maybe she should have come in winter, when the vegetation had died down. Holywell Cemetery was designated a wildlife sanctuary, a euphemism for overgrown, and just getting to the graves was a struggle.

Just then she heard a cough. She looked round but there was no-one there. It must have been more wildlife, she decided, and continued with her search. Alice had seen a plan of the graves in the City Library so she knew she was in the right place. She was looking for an ancestor; quite a character, by all accounts, and something of an inventor too.

Alice was not the kind of person to get easily spooked, but as she moved from headstone to headstone, she began to get an eerie feeling that someone was watching her.

'Don't be ridiculous,' she told herself. The Law Library was not far away and the Science Area just up the road. These solid institutions of rational, uncompromising certainty reassured her, and she concentrated on pulling one last bramble from a grave which might, just might, be the one she was looking for. With a jerk it came free. Another disappointment.

Suddenly she felt a chill down her spine. There was no doubt about it now: she was not alone. Cautiously she looked round and saw a thin, slight figure, silhouetted between the yew trees.

'My dear young lady. I hope I haven't alarmed you,' said the figure, in a lofty tone.

'No . . . no,' stammered Alice.

There was a pause. Then he said, 'Do you happen to have the time?'

Alice looked at her watch. 'It's ten to twelve.'

'How interesting. I've always been interested in time.' The stranger had a very pronounced nose, a receding chin, and a tall black hat pushed back on his head. He looked rather odd, Alice thought, but so did a lot of people in Oxford, and they were usually harmless.

The stranger seemed to be waiting for Alice to speak, so she said, 'I'm looking for a grave.'

'There's plenty here.'

'The man I'm looking for was interested in time too,' said Alice. 'He invented an alarm clock.'

'A man of genius,' said the stranger.

'He was my great, great grandfather.'

'You must be very proud of him. He's over there, next to those angels.'

She went over to where the man pointed – and there it was. 'In Loving Memory of Theophilus Carter. Rest in Peace.' A very plain grave for a genius.

'How did you know who I was looking for?' Alice asked.

'There are many geniuses here, but only one of them invented an alarm clock.' There was another pause before the stranger observed, 'At half past three it's time for tea; at ten to four it's time for more.' Then he added, 'It was more of a bed than an alarm clock. It tipped you onto the floor to wake you up.'

'Yes – I had heard about that. It sounds quite dangerous,' said Alice.

'You are a very perceptive young lady.'

'Was it really displayed at the Great Exhibition?' she asked.

'It was. Then in the window of 48 High Street for the

good citizens of Oxford to admire.'

Another awkward silence followed until the stranger said, 'Five and twenty to eight is an interesting time. You are either getting ready for breakfast or getting ready for dinner.' Then, rather as an afterthought, 'It was called Carter's Clockwork Bed.'

The city clocks began to chime. It took a full five minutes before they were all finished. 'Twelve o' clock!' the stranger said. 'A very interesting time. Oxford can never make up its mind when it is.'

'Do you think he invented anything else?' asked Alice.

'Oh yes, a great many things – a very great many.' He shook his head, sadly.

'What sort of things?'

'Carter's Revolving Milk Jug, Carter's Automatic Shoe Polisher, Carter's Illuminating Umbrella. Many, many contributions to the advancement of civilisation and the comfort of mankind. But today only his image is remembered, and there was so much more to the man, so much . . .,' he sighed.

'His image?'

'And what's worse – it's been usurped as fiction. It's little short of scandalous.'

'Where can I find out more about him?' Alice asked. 'They don't have any information in the Bodleian.'

But the stranger seemed to ignore her as he pulled out a large pocket watch, shook it and held it to his ear.

Then muttering 'Look at the time, the time, the time . . .' he hurried off towards St Cross Road.

Alice was determined not to let him get away. 'Wait for me!' she called. But by the time she had got to the cemetery gate, he had disappeared. Then she heard a squealing of brakes and angry shouting and, in the distance she saw a tall black hat bobbing towards Long Wall Street.

Alice was a fast walker, but she couldn't catch up with him. A throng of Spanish schoolchildren blocked her view, but then she saw the hat again, turning into High Street. There was no sign of him when she got there and, frustrated, she walked up towards Queens Lane, looking to right and left. Suddenly she saw him, standing outside a shoe-shop. It was number 48, the very shop that had once been owned by her great, great grandfather.

He glanced at Alice and walked inside, with Alice following only moments later.

Shoes, boots and belts lined the walls, together with a good selection of Oxford souvenirs for the tourist trade. But apart from the assistant, she was alone in the shop.

'Can I help you?' asked the assistant.

'Where's the man who came in just now?'

'No-one's been in here for half an hour.'

'Are you sure? I've just seen him.'

'Quite sure, but you are welcome to look around.'

On the back wall a framed and faded photograph caught her eye. It was of this same shop, taken long ago.

The name was just readable: 'Theo Carter, Furnisher to the Gentry and University'. In front of it stood the proprietor, a character with a very pronounced nose, receding chin and a tall black hat pushed back on his head. He looked remarkably like . . . Alice felt a chill down her spine again . . . exactly like the man she met in the cemetery. Turning, she saw him again – on a range of T-shirts decorated with characters from Alice's Adventures in Wonderland.

A sensible, level-headed girl like Alice didn't believe in ghosts of course but, as she left the shop, she smiled at the thought that her great, great grandfather must have been the original Mad Hatter.

❧⟡⟐⟡☙

*The 1881 census shows that Theophilus Carter lived over the shop at 48 High Street with his wife, daughter, granddaughter and two servants, and that he employed five men in his furnishing business. He did indeed invent a clockwork bed which tipped its occupant onto the floor at the appointed hour, and it was exhibited at the Great Exhibition of 1851. He became one of Oxford's well-known eccentrics and stories about him were being exchanged long after his death. In March 1931 The Times published correspondence from those who claimed to have known him, including the Rev. Gordon Baillie, who wrote: 'All Oxford called him The Mad Hatter. He would stand at the door of his furniture shop in the High, always with a top hat at the back of his head which, with a well-developed nose and a somewhat receding chin, made him an easy target for the caricaturist.' It is widely believed that Lewis Carroll, the pen-name of the Christ Church mathematician who wrote Alice's Adventures in Wonderland, not only used him as his inspiration for The Mad*

*Hatter, but commissioned Sir John Tenniel to draw him for the book.*

*Number 48 High Street is currently occupied by Fitrite Shoes. Previous tenants have included William Morris, who ran his bicycle repair business from these premises before branching out into car production, an industry which dominated Oxford's economy for much of the twentieth century.*

# *Tiger Lily*

## *Nichola May*

Thomas Madison Browning had long intended to give up smoking, but women – or rather one woman – was making it impossible.

Every Friday, after filing papers in his briefcase, he would stroll out to savor the two loves of his life: Cohiba Exquisito cigars and the woman who sold them.

He studied her hands, a ring on every finger, as she passed the cigars across the counter.

'Bells on her toes,' Thomas said out loud.

'Sorry?' 'The rhyme, you know:

*Ride-a-cock-horse to Banbury Cross,*

*to see a fine lady upon a white horse,*

*with rings on her fingers and bells on her toes,*

*she shall have music wherever she goes.'*

She smiled. 'You're funny.'

Thomas had never been called funny before.

One Friday afternoon, as she served him, her blouse slipped and she revealed a shoulder. 'It's a tiger, can you tell?' she said. 'Had it done at the tattoo shop next door. I do so love a man with a tattoo.'

'A-a-a.' Thomas said, then closed his mouth and left without taking his change.

Thomas took Monday morning off work. He sat down among the nose rings, fluorescent hair spray, hookah pipes and leather corsets.

It was only a small design, a woman on a horse.

'I'd like a name on it,' Thomas said. The tattooist obliged. Thomas winced.

'Popular name,' said the tattooist, helping Thomas on with his shirt, 'you're the third bloke this week wanting that. If she's anything as great as my Lily, then good luck to you.'

'Your Lily?'

◈

*Tiger Lily is an alternative clothes store/piercing and tattoo studio based in New Inn Hall Street. Until 2010 the newsagents just around the corner in New Road sold cigars (including Cohiba Exquisito) from a humidor on their shop counter. 'Ride-a-Cock Horse' is a traditional nursery rhyme that originated in the nearby town of Banbury.*

# At Her Table

## *Wendy Greenberg*

Erica hadn't told anyone that Thom and Myra were back in town. She had seen them yesterday as she was escaping from the heat of the day into the chilled stone larder that was the Covered Market, a bewitching cornucopia of foodie delights.

Shoppers had bustled around her and she dodged out of the crowd to catch her breath under the awning of the organic meat shop. The sleek pelts of slaughtered wild animals hung unapologetically over the entrance advertising the carnivorous wares. Butcher and daughter were busy attempting to unhook the delivery bicycle which was suspended high above the side of the shop, unseen by the hoi polloi. High rise bicycle parking bays. The tall pole with its hook swung like a seafront game back and forth, in ever more desperate attempts to unhook the bike.

At 'The Cake Shop' a team of steady-handed women had toiled in their white overalls, expertly creating custom-made characters for the magnificent celebration cakes. Huge wedding cakes of top-table guests copied from photographs to mimic the real event, mind-numbing chocolate creations awesome in their attention to detail, layers of white iced fruit cakes bedecked with crimson hand-made rosebuds. Faces of passers-by squashed against the windows watching this fascinating assembly line.

Erica had been with the greengrocer who was filling her bag with local new potatoes when a familiar voice made her turn. It was him – Thom Denby!

Still slim hipped, he was brushing his thick, now silvering curls back from his smiling face, his voice as mesmerising and seductive as ever. Her heart missed a beat and she dropped her bag.

'Everything OK love?' the stallholder asked.

Thom's voice had stunned her. She watched, holding her breath, as the potatoes rolled towards him. Thom looked down to see what had hit him then he glanced in her direction, narrowing his meltingly brown eyes. He paused before hesitantly kicking his small football out of the way and turned. He walked a few paces and looked back over his shoulder.

Next day, as Erica sat in the morning sunshine half awake, half dozing, she tried to plan the menu. Tonight Erica and Fraser were expecting the usual crowd. The familiar recipe book now lay in her lap. The food, she needed to focus on the food . . . but she could not stop thinking about Thom.

She imagined the spread she would make. Large oil-drenched green olives nestling beside chunks of preserved tangy lemon, warm sun-ripened tomatoes, piercingly hot chillies stuffed with crumbly, salty feta and artichokes, their layers lying opened, exposed, full, lush and smoky. All served with warm foccacia bread to soak up the tangy flavours.

Thom had made her laugh in the way that Myra had laughed yesterday, as she nestled into Thom's shoulder. He had held Erica like that once, his voice whispering deep in her ear, vibrating every nerve, caressing her senses.

She had thought the madness of that summer was long over.

She would roast a couple of chickens with herbs. Massaged with pungent, peppery Sicilian olive oil, stuffed with rosemary and thyme and served with some small, crisp potatoes sizzling and appetizing, dusted in Maldon sea salt with whole roasted bulbs of green garlic, layers of roasted Mediterranean vegetables and some crisp salad leaves. This gutsy feast would be washed down by smooth Italian Montepulciano or hearty Spanish Rioja.

But she could not concentrate. She was being flooded with long exiled memories. Her body was being aroused with the past. She leant back and slowly fingered the old book still lying across her bare legs. She carelessly turned the worn pages, food stains reminding her of parties past, dinners prepared, friends and neighbours entertained, late night arguments and embraces. She loved her life. She had thought passion was over. She looked, self-consciously, down on her middle-aged form.

Dessert, what would they have for dessert? The silky coconut crème caramel that slipped onto the palate and slid down slowly, its flavours unfolding down your throat, or should it be nectarines baked with honey and crushed ginger biscuits served at blood temperature with a whipped cream cheese – or sweet, ripe oranges sliced with the oozing seeds from the wizened husks of the spent passion fruit?

For a moment Erica found herself yearning to be preparing this feast for Thom. When would she share the news of Thom and Myra's return? How would they react? Maybe she would wait until she prepared the rich dark arabica coffee they all loved, steamed through the old coffee maker and, as the aromatic promise was released into the room, she could begin to pick over old wounds. It could be a little something extra to serve up alongside the oak-aged Armagnac and bitter mints. Or she could say nothing.

*The Covered Market can be accessed from High Street, Cornmarket Street or Market Street. In the 18th century the streets of Oxford were becoming increasingly congested on market days as market stalls interfered with traffic. So, in 1774, a new market for vegetables, meat and fish was built. John Gwynn, the architect of Magdalen Bridge, drew up the plans and designed the High Street front with its four entrances. The earliest stalls were in colonnaded blocks: the high-raftered roofs of today are the result of 19th century development.*

*The Covered Market is home to numerous traders selling a variety of goods: fresh fruit, vegetables, breads and cakes, meats, cheeses, seafood, fine foods, flowers, leather goods, shoes, jewellery and clothing. The Cake Shop's wedding cakes have been feted by You & Your Wedding magazine which puts two of their cakes in the Top 10 Most Amazing Wedding Cakes. The shop takes special commissions and takes great pride in its attention to detail. A replica of the Radcliffe Camera took 80 hours to make and assemble. Steps were counted to match the real building and even the numbers of bars on the windows were checked and all details made to scale. The most expensive cake the team has designed and created cost £2600 and depicted an Inca Temple.*

*Oxford's Covered Market is open seven days a week, 8.30– 17.30 Monday to Saturday and 10.00–16.00 Sundays. Shop for Erica's dinner. Find the hidden bicycle parking for the butchers. You could also look for the greengrocers, Italian deli, coffee shop and cheese stall where Erica purchased the ingredients for her feast.*

# *The Road Not Taken*

## *Jackie Vickers*

I love everything about this place.

I love its modest classical exterior, its peaceful, unassuming interior.

I once heard a tourist complain that this building was uninteresting. 'Compare this with the elaborate church interiors of the same period in Bavaria,' he said crossly to his companion, 'or the beautiful ornamentation of the French or Italian Baroque. There is nothing to look at here.'

You have missed the point, I wanted to say. You mistake simplicity for plain-ness.

Every year I buy my season ticket for the Sunday morning Coffee Concerts. The music is always wonderful, but I also enjoy the historic associations, for the Holywell Music Room was the first purpose-built concert hall in Europe and is still in continuous use for recitals and concerts.

But is there more to my attachment to this building than Sunday music in an historic venue? Of course there is.

This Sunday, for the first time, I have brought my young daughter, who already shows promise on the violin. As we are early, I tell her some of the history of this place and that gentlemen were asked not to bring their dogs into the concerts here. I tell her about the uproar when the leader's violin was broken by an orange, thrown with force from the audience. She is excited and full of questions. Then the rustling and whispering stops and is followed by a murmur of disappointment at the announcement that the soloist has been taken ill, and there will be a few changes to the programme. The replacement emerges from the door behind us and comes forward, smiling, to acknowledge the applause and I am deafened by the roaring in my ears from my own heartbeats. The performer steps back and leans over her violin for a final tuning. Her thick dark red hair hangs over her face as she adjusts the pegs, then she flicks her hair back and fiddles with the scarf she wears under her violin in place of a shoulder rest. After a short pause, she draws the bow across the strings with a graceful arm movement. And the first notes of the Bach B minor sonata fill the room.

Fleur Fleming looks exactly as I remember her, though her playing has acquired more emotional depth in the last fifteen years. When the applause for the Bach dies away she announces the first programme change and I now know that she has seen me, for it is the Telemann E minor sonata. And I am immediately transported to that terrible afternoon in my rooms and the last time she had played this piece for me.

We had met the summer before I came up to Oxford to read music. I was queuing for a Prom ticket, outside the Albert Hall, when Fleur fell over my feet. That's all it takes, one small collision to alter the course of a life.

The first thing I noticed was her long red hair, then her graceful movements and laughing green eyes.

She said the first thing she noticed about me was my feet.

What do I remember about that first summer in London with Fleur? Certain moments stand out, the steady ominous pulse of the slow movement of Beethoven's Seventh on our first date at the Festival Hall. The sweet melancholy flute melody of Gluck's 'Dance of the Blessed Spirits' at a lunch-time recital at St Martin in the Fields. A military band playing in the park as we sheltered under trees during a shower. But of the things that mattered the most to me, only the taste of her skin and the memory of the weight of her hair in my hands, remains.

I remember her mounting excitement as October and her second year at the Guildhall School of Music approached and my sadness at our unavoidable separation. She had heard there were to be staff changes, and spent feverish hours setting before me the relative reputations of the remaining teachers and what this might mean. In the end it was only rumour and she soon moved on to concerns about her violin and its possible shortcomings in the upper register. Difficult times, as I tried to calm her apprehensions and attend to my own.

Then term started and we began, inevitably, to see less of each other, though we managed to meet most weekends. If a musical event was timetabled for a Saturday evening, Fleur would catch the last train, to be with me by midnight. We would get up late and race across the parks and up Holywell Street in time for a Coffee Concert. Later she would play her current studies to me, anything from Mozart to John Adams. She was already showing a preference for the Baroque and always ended with some Bach or Corelli, which I believed would be retained for ever in some storage facility of my mind. The holidays were long and we still managed afternoons on the river, picnics in the woods and music-making with our friends, but for Fleur, set on a performing career, there were also hours and hours of practice.

But I had assumed too much and when the hammer blow came it was far worse for being unexpected. We were walking back through the parks after our Sunday morning concert and I was talking about finals, which were only weeks away, when Fleur, who clearly had not heard a word, told me that she had been offered a place at the Juilliard School.

'New York!' I had said.

She was dancing with excitement. 'Think what it means!'

But I could only think that she had gone to New York for an audition and had never told me. I had become fixed on the how and the where, like someone who has just heard of their partner's infidelity and repeatedly returns to details of the time and the place.

For more than two years we had made music and made love and it often seemed like the same thing. I had been enchanted by her loveliness and her talent and it suddenly came to me that I had been drifting uncritically in her wake. And even then, despite this unwelcome discovery that her charisma cloaked a blazing determination, I could not really believe her ambition would destroy my dream of a steady job, a place in an orchestra for Fleur, and a modest house in a leafy road filled with children and music. But Fleur would have none of it. Nothing less than the world stage would do. We argued for hours. Fleur talked of the reputation of the Juilliard teachers, the standard of the other students and the guarantee of a future on the concert platform.

I disagreed. 'No-one can guarantee your future as a soloist.'

'America is the land of the possible.'

I remember pleading my own case, a contact already made with a music publisher.

'You expect me to give up my chance for your job. With a music publisher!' she said dismissively.

'You'd be happy playing from manuscript, I suppose.'

'Well, Bach managed!'

And so it went on all afternoon, from bad-tempered bickering to tears and shouting on her part and mutism on mine. In truth I would not give up the promise of a secure future in a city I loved, for an unknown number of years dancing attendance on Fleur. In the end there was no more to say. I think we both knew this was our last afternoon together and all our love and regret seemed encapsulated in her faultless rendering of our current favourite, the Telemann E minor sonata.

Why should this sorry tale be any different from any other love affair gone sour from a familiar mix of young love, immaturity, ambition and selfishness? Would a more determined or experienced couple have known how to negotiate those obstacles of time and place? She sent letters from America full of what I saw as facile declarations. Eventually I tied the letters up and hid them, with my memories, under my socks.

A small elbow nudges my arm and I join in the clapping. It is painful leaving my memories of the cluttered student room where I had lain on the rumpled sheets on our last afternoon, enveloped in the rise and fall of that Telemann sonata.

The room empties and now that I stand close to her I see there have been changes, after all. There are fine lines around her eyes and deeper ones by her mouth.

'A fine performance,' I say.

'Thank you. I had forgotten how good the acoustics are here.' The old energy and sparkle has diminished, she seems tired.

'You never came back to Oxford,' I say quietly, trying not to make it sound like an accusation.

'I heard you were married.'

Fleur stands at the back of the stage by her violin case and its precious contents, the Guarnerius loaned by the Guildhall, which she always keeps within reach. She slackens her bow and clips it into the case and I see there are no rings on her long slender fingers. The violin lies there, wrapped in the red silk scarf she still uses to protect her collar bone. I recognise it as my last gift to her.

'The colour hasn't faded,' I say, hoping to get beyond our cool meaningless exchanges.

'Some things don't.' She avoids my gaze and looks across to the entrance where my young daughter is eagerly sifting through CDs for sale.

I follow her glance. 'I don't think she'll find anything she doesn't already have. She's a great fan of your Baroque Ensemble. You have quite a reputation now,' I add, 'recitals, recordings, visiting professor at Milan . . .' and I realise, too late, that she will know now how closely I have followed her success.

She nods. 'Are you busy?'

I don't answer.

'Music publishing is satisfying?' she persists.

'The children are musical,' I say, to change the subject.

'Children?'

'My son shows promise on the keyboard. But he's young and still fidgets. I'll bring him next year.'

'And your wife?' Fleur snaps her case shut and zips up the outer cover. She turns, but I can't hold her gaze.

'She plays the oboe,' I say, deliberately misunderstanding.

Fleur looks at my child as she runs across waving a CD. There is an intensity to Fleur's expression that I have only seen once, on our last afternoon together, when she spoke of the Juilliard, and her future.

'I hear you play the violin too.' She leans forward. 'What's your name?' I draw my daughter towards me and hold her closely.

'Fleur,' I say, 'her name is Fleur.'

❧🙰🙰☙

*The Holywell Music Room, built in 1742, is the oldest purpose-built music room in Europe and therefore England's first concert hall. Many musicians, including Haydn, have performed here. Coffee Concerts, established more than twenty years ago, are held here nearly every Sunday morning in addition to regular concerts and occasional free lunch-time recitals.*

# *Personation*

## *Kathleen Daly*

6 May 2010. Spring. But this is Oxford, and a northerly wind chills the streets and creeps under doors like a stray cat. I emerge from my day in the dark underbelly of the Radcliffe Camera. Beyond the pierced nipple of its dome, the sky is darkening. I cough out the book dust clogging my throat. Thank the powers that be for the advent of the internet. Soon I'll be able to consult all the books I want, without leaving my college basement just across the square. I adjust my polaroids, to screen out the sodium glow thrown up from the cobbles of Radcliffe Square. My night is beginning.

I get a real buzz from the atmosphere of Election Night just before the polls close. Tonight will be the night my X will be the last in the ballot box. I watch the last stragglers exit the polling booth, and make my entry a few minutes before 10. A very superior woman with a tight blue-rinse perm hands me two slips.

'Now, you put the yellow slip in the box with the

yellow label, and the white slip in the box with the white label.'

'Thank you so much, I'd never have guessed.'

'Only one cross on each ballot paper.'

'How disappointing, I thought I could vote for all the candidates.'

She scrutinises me over her owlish specs, then frowns with glee.

'Could you repeat your name?' I do so.

'I need to draw your attention to the "Summary of corrupt and illegal practices at elections for the guidance of voters." '

'Oh,' I say. 'Why?'

'Per-son-ation.'

'Never heard of it.'

She points to the notices pinned up round the polling booths, and chants :

' "A person shall for all purposes of the laws relating to local government elections be deemed guilty of the offences of person-at-ion at a local government election if he b) votes in person or proxy; subsection (i) for a person whom he knows or has reasonable grounds for supposing to be dead or ... a fictitious person." '

I recoil.

'Look, it's now five to ten. I need to vote. What's the problem?'

'I think you are guilty of personation!' she crows.

This is too much.

'I've voted in person at every election since the Great Reform Act. What's more, the Inland Revenue are still sending me tax forms. Dear Lady, I am Count Dracula.'

She sniffs. 'Well, I don't believe you. Those canines are false.'

'Madam, even vampires need a dentist after half a millenium!'

'I can't allow you to cast a vote that's potentially illegal.'

The clock of St Mary the Virgin chimes ten. I was so near to being the last voter. Next moonless night, I'll show her 'personation'. Just now, I won't give her the pleasure of the last word.

'Never mind, my chick,' I purr, 'I have all the time in the world. And the next election is sooner than you think!'

୬ଧଠ୫୭

*Most names and locations in this story have been concealed to protect identities (especially that of Dracula's College). Radcliffe Square is a magnet for visitors, set between the ancient church St Mary the Virgin, All Souls and Brasenose Colleges, and the walls of the Old Bodleian. Its centrepiece is the dome of the Radcliffe Camera.*

# *Marble*
## *Janet Bolam*

***B**oyle's Law: The pressure of a given quantity of gas varies inversely as its volume at constant temperature*

'Ah, Geoff,' the new Headmaster indicated a seat in the corner of his study. The man hardly knows me and he calls me Geoff. Even Andrea, my wife, may she rest in peace, always called me Geoffrey.

' I expect you have lots of plans to fill up your retired days?' He was all joviality.

'Yes, Headmaster, but that isn't for another four terms.'

'Of course,' the Headmaster shuffled slightly, avoiding eye contact, 'that is what I wanted to discuss with you.' He was clearly uncomfortable. 'As you know, we are introducing a number of changes to the running of the school, and it has come to my notice that you are rather…struggling…with them.'

I stared at him over my glasses. Was this little pipsqueak planning to discipline me?

'If you mean the relaxing of our discipline policies, yes, I do disagree with you. I have had nearly forty years experience teaching, most of it in this school and I know from bitter experience...'

'Let's not revisit this particular topic, Geoff, except to say that we have had yet another complaint, this time from Simpson Minor's parents.' The Headmaster stood abruptly and turned to look out of the window. 'We need to introduce change, to progress. It was after all, why I was appointed.' He allowed a silence to develop, then he returned to his seat. 'I have a proposal to put to you.'

I settled my hands on my lap and composed my face.

'It is of course entirely your decision, but would you consider taking early retirement?' The Headmaster was now staring at a point on the back of his hands. I wasn't sure I'd heard correctly. 'Naturally,' he hurried on, 'we would ensure you had a fitting send off, and of course, there would be no adverse impact on your pension.' As the silence drew on, he rose hesitantly from his seat, indicating the door.

'No pressure. Just give it some thought?'

I do not remember the journey back to my flat. I was in shock. I stared out over the quad, the familiar view of the Porter's lodge and the Wiltshire hills beyond. I had taught physics in this school for my whole career, and to be summarily dismissed... I poured myself a large brandy. Of course, I had to leave as soon as I could. To stay any longer would be insupportable. No pressure indeed.

I left at the end of term, a year earlier than I had planned. For the first time I could remember, I had time on my hands. It yawned in front of me like a huge cavern, sat on my shoulders reminding me that I was totally unprepared for this idleness, this time when my life was not regulated by classes and bells. I resolved to keep busy. After all, I reasoned, I was not the first person to find themselves unexpectedly retired.

Firmly, I turned my attention to the matter of accommodation. To stay with my daughter would be inappropriate. She had rather haltingly offered when it first became clear that I needed temporary accommodation, but even taking into account the slight thaw in our relationship of late, I knew I would not be welcome. I moved into a B&B whilst I considered my options. I decided to explore possibilities in Oxford, and an ideal opportunity presented itself when my granddaughter Emma asked me to accompany her to an Oxford University Open Day.

Oxford was at its best in the sunshine and Emma was animated, a constant stream of excited babble, reminding me so much of her grandmother. We fell into old ways as I quizzed her on the evidence Darwin had collected in order to formulate his theory of Evolution, as arm-in-arm, we crossed the road to visit the Botanic Garden. I had not anticipated the river, which we came across rather suddenly as we turned from one of the glasshouses. It was covered in punts, earnest tourists and careless students. Why people are entertained by pushing a boat along some water with a stick eludes me. My eye fell upon a giddy girl who was teetering on the edge of a boat, waving wildly towards the bank. She was so frantic that I feared she would fall into the river until I realised she was waving to Emma who started waving back, jumping up and down. We watched the punt wobble its way to the shore.

'Emma! Is it you? Why, didn't you tell me you were coming?'

'Molly! I thought you would be doing exams or something?'

'Finished ages ago! We're having a picnic and Tim is trying to convince us of his manhood.' She brazenly tapped Tim's bared calf with her foot as he self-consciously planted the pole vertically into the riverbed and grinned.

'Why don't you jump in? There's plenty of room.'

I saw Emma's eyes light up before she stopped herself. 'I'm not sure,' she mumbled, throwing a quick glance in my direction.

I cleared my throat, ready to refuse their kind invitation, but Molly pushed on.

'We'll only be an hour!'

There was an awkward silence.

'Of course you must go, Emma,' I heard myself saying. 'I am perfectly happy to have a short wander around. I'll meet you outside University College at two-thirty. But don't be late.'

As I watched them disappear under Magdalen Bridge, the sounds of their laughter echoing off its walls, I was surprised at how sad and disappointed I felt. I took a deep breath and with a glance at my watch, I wandered slowly along High Street, where a plaque on the wall caught my eye. Not the usual blue plaque, but a grey rectangle that contrasted with the golden stone in which it was embedded. I stopped to read it.

**In a house on this site, between 1655 and 1668 lived**
**ROBERT BOYLE**
**Here he discovered BOYLE'S LAW and made experiments with an**
**AIR PUMP designed by his assistant, ROBERT HOOKE,**
**Inventor Scientist and Architect who made a MICROSCOPE**
**and thereby first identified the LIVING CELL**

Then, quite out of nowhere, I remembered I had been here before. I had stood before this very plaque as a boy of perhaps fifteen. A wave of nostalgia ran through me. Mr Kramer. I saw him standing where I was standing now, Panama hat tipped backwards, shirt sleeves rolled up, arms waving lazily in the air as he explained the importance of Boyle's Law and the brilliance of Hooke. We boys stood with rapt attention. Mr Kramer came from Florida and rumour had it that he was a former fighter pilot who had been involved in the early space programme. He certainly knew all about satellites and rocketry, and it was because of him that I traced Explorer and Sputnik events in minute detail. I smiled at my childhood dreams of going to the USA and working on the space programme. It was why I chose to study physics at university. I looked back at the plaque, remembering the feeling of optimism, of unbounded possibilities, the excitement, that I had felt that day. The sharp feeling of failure that shot through me took me rather by surprise.

'Look at you now!' a voice in my head crushed me. 'You are a sad diminished old man! What happened to you? Once, you wanted to be an astronaut!'

**Boyle's Law: *if you increase the pressure, the volume gets less***

The entrance to University College was unremarkable, as was the quad immediately inside, but there was an interesting door in the corner that led to a domed room, stars painted above, an elaborate plinth below, and an astonishing white marble figure of a naked man lying on his side, head thrown back, mouth open, vulnerable. There was something voyeuristic, disturbing, as if I was watching the dying gasps of this drowning man, his agony frozen in time.

Percy Bysshe Shelley
Born Aug 4th 1792
Died July 8th 1822

Transfixed, my eyes lifted to see a verse written on the wall.

'A heart grown cold, a head grown grey in vain;

Nor, when the spirit's self has ceased to burn,

With sparkless ashes load an unlamented urn.'

I don't know how long I stood there. Somehow, a gate within me had opened, and feelings and thoughts I had held at bay for years began to flood into the vacuum, unmerciful, unedited. The memory of Andrea fighting to surface the water, gasping for breath, of me holding out a branch, 'Grab onto this!' of me jumping into the fast moving river and searching for her. I couldn't see anything except turbulent water. I kept surfacing and calling her name, but she was gone.

Cold, failed, friendless, all humanity banished for fear of feeling too much, I have become like this statue, a man of marble. 'A heart grown cold, a head grown grey in vain.' I tried to re-establish my equilibrium but I couldn't stop myself from shaking. The room around me, the people, seemed to sway, sounds came to me as if I was underwater, I was struggling to breathe, filled with a fear that I was going to faint and make a spectacle of myself. A hand on my arm. A young man was looking at me with concern. Was I alright? Could he lead me to the nearby bench to sit?

'It's Mr Metcalf isn't it? Do you remember me?' he said.

I nodded and smiled politely, trying to work out who he was. He brought me a glass of water and sat on the bench next to me.

'I run a lab in California now. Institute of Deep Sea Research ... you may have heard of us?'

I went on nodding, hoping I would eventually remember who he was, but it continued to elude me. He was laughing nervously, saying something about a Conference, then he was gone. I remembered his name was Greaves, one of so many faceless boys sitting along brown benches, working their way through Boyle's Law.

**Boyle's Law: We normally don't feel the pressure of the atmosphere on us because the human body is primarily**

*made up of liquid, and liquids are non compressible*

But what if you are drowning, locked in a deep and cold and compressed place? What happens to the human body then? I found unbidden tears running down my face.

Emma found me still seated. She was radiant, pink from running to meet me on time. She put her arms around my neck and kissed my cheek.

'Shall we take a look at the Bod?' she smiled, and a flicker of warmth began to move through me. I looked up to the surface and let the water gently push me towards the sun.

∽৪০৫৪∾

*The Shelley Memorial is dedicated to the poet Percy Bysshe Shelley (1792–1822) at University College, Oxford, England, the college that he briefly attended and from which he was expelled for writing a pamphlet, 'The Necessity of Atheism'. Although Shelley was expelled from the college, he remains one of its most famous alumni and is now held in high honour there.*

*The statue was commissioned by Shelley's daughter-in-law, Lady Shelley. It was originally intended to be located in the Protestant Cemetery in Rome where Shelley is buried, at the request of adventurer Edward John Trelawney, a friend of Shelley. Trelawney wanted to have a monument of the poet next to his own. However, Trelawney's descendants thought that Shelley's statue was too large, and thus did not consent to his wishes. Eventually the statue ended up at University College, donated by Lady Shelley, with a formal opening ceremony on 14 June 1893.*

*The Shelley Memorial is located on the site where the scientists Robert Boyle and Robert Hooke performed experiments while they were in Oxford, known as Cross Hall until the early 1800s. This is recorded for passers-by on a plaque on the exterior wall of the memorial in the High Street. According to Boyle's Law, the pressure of a given quantity of gas varies inversely as its volume at constant temperature.*

# Buckland and the Elephant

## S. A. Edwards

A handbill found crumpled on the floor of the Eagle and Child:

### Bostock and Wombwell's Beast Show

*Amongst the Number of Natural Curiosities arrived in this City, there seems none to equal or rival the wonderful elephant Esmerelda. Those Ladies and Gentlemen who have already seen this extraordinary pachyderm, are so highly gratified with the sight, that the Proprietor flatters himself, from their high recommendation that all ranks of people will gratify their curiosity, as she is undoubtedly the only one of her kind ever exhibited in the kingdom alive.*

### To be seen at St Giles Fair, St Giles Oxford
### September 1st 1845

'Roll up, roll up. For only three pence you can see her enormous ears, gaze into her ancient eyes and for an extra penny you can feed her a bun. Imagine, Ladies and Gentlemen, the sensation of her trunk as she takes the bun from your fingers. Dare you Sir?'

Mr Bostock the joint owner of Bostock and Wombwell's Beast Show was working the crowd. Inside the stiflingly hot canvas awning, Esmerelda the elephant swayed from side to side. The crowd queued patiently, waiting to be ushered in for their audience with the animal. The canvas flaps were lifted and they moved into the gloom of the tent.

'Cor she stinks. Take a whiff of that, Ma,' shrieked a small ginger-haired boy as Esmerelda lifted her tail and defecated.

'That's a massive one. Your dad would only need one of those for the whole allotment,' observed the child's mother.

'Go on then, mate. I'll give you a penny to feed it,' shouted a young man egged on to bravery by his girlfriend.

The elephant raised her sad eyes and with infinite gentleness took the bun from his outstretched hand. She waved the bun above the heads of the crowd before twisting her trunk and popping the bun into her mouth. The crowd roared with laughter.

'Me next, me next,' called the ginger-haired boy, elbowing his way to the front of the bun queue.

The Very Reverend William Buckland, Canon of Christ Church observed to his wife that he had rung three times and no tea had yet arrived.

'It's that blasted Fair,' she replied. 'The maid has the day off to go gallivanting. I'll fetch your tea'. She stumbled over the tortoise as she left the room.

Dr Buckland's study contained almost as many live specimens as dead ones. The tortoise lived under the sideboard. A ring-necked parakeet sat on a stand by the window. A gecko rolled its eyes from a glass tank. Every surface of Buckland's study was covered in shells, bones, fossils, minerals, stones, books and half eaten bits of toast. In the centre of this organised chaos sat Dr Buckland with an enormous ginger cat on his knee. His black ecclesiastical robes gave him the appearance of a necromancer. He rubbed the cat affectionately under the chin and it blinked its green eyes at him in appreciation.

'The Fair' he mused to the cat 'I haven't been for years. I think I would like to go.' The cat feigned interest then looked disgruntled as it was pitched off his knee.

Dr Buckland was a zoophagist. His ambition was to eat his way, for scientific research, through the animal kingdom. While younger men were arguing about Darwin's new theories of evolution, Buckland was eating his way through bluebottles, crocodiles, moles, bats, beetles.

He had started his hobby by trying to eat his way through the animal world in alphabetical order. When aardvark proved too difficult to source he decided to eat what came available and simply to chart his progress through the different species, sub-species and genera, with tasting notes. His rooms in Christ Church were decorated with the skeletal remains of his most interesting meals, mounted in life-like poses.

'We'll move her after dark,' said Mr Bostock. 'I don't

want no-one getting a look at her for free'.

The elephant's chain was unbolted from its stake and with sharp pokes behind her ears to encourage her, she was walked across the town to the Christ Church meadows where the rest of the Beast Show was camped. The animal moved slowly and shook her head from side to side.

'She don't look well, Boss' said one of the costermongers.

A jet of green, stinking faeces exploded from her and spattered all over Mr Bostock's trousers.

'Shit' he said.

As the sun rose over the Isis and the mist of morning evaporated away, Esmerelda the elephant died.

Dr Buckland whistled as he walked to the Beast Show camp. The rat tucked inside his hassock fidgeted and stuck its nose out of the vestments to see where they were. 'Stop that! It tickles,' The Very Reverend remonstrated. 'Excuse me young man, I would like to see the elephant.'

'Miss, if you don't mind' said Consuela, the Bearded Lady, 'Better ask the boss, that's him over there. I don't know how much he's going to charge to see a dead one. Can't imagine there's going to be much demand myself.'

Buckland's heart missed a beat.

'Dead?' He almost sprinted over to Mr Bostock. 'When did it die?' he asked.

'Bloody hell. Have you come to give it the Last

Rites?' said Mr Bostock.

'No, no, no. I would like to buy the carcass,' said Buckland.

Mr Bostock stopped looking depressed and started to look shifty.

'Well, that's a very valuable bit of meat, that is. How much is it worth to you?'

Buckland threw caution to the wind and said with great aplomb 'Three shillings and six pence.'

'You are taking the mickey, Reverend. I could feed the lions for a month on Esmerelda. I need at least ten guineas to make it worth my while.'

'I'll pay you eleven including delivery' said Buckland, who was warming to the art of negotiation.

There was a tricky moment as they negotiated the gate into Tom Quad in Christ Church college, but with a lot of shoving and pushing, the late Esmerelda eventually popped like a cork out of a bottle on to the grass.

Now Buckland had his elephant, how was he to cook it? His scientific mind turned hypotheses and parameters, paradigms and conjectures till his synapses ached. If he was successful who would remember Darwin with his ridiculous new ideas? It would be Buckland's name that would echo down the ages. Cheered by this thought he set to work. So what to do? He wrote and drew till the cat thoroughly exasperated got off his knee and went to sit on its own, throwing him the occasional dirty look.

1.  He could joint the carcass and cook it in pieces, but no, he knew the college butcher – Mr Grimshaw

wouldn't have a chopper big enough.

2.   He could wrap it in pastry. Elephant pie. He didn't like pie.

3.   He could cover it in breadcrumbs. He didn't have a dish big enough to roll it in.

Buckland was beginning to feel dispirited.

'You could roast it' his wife suggested bringing him more tea and toast, 'but you will have to keep the meat moist. You don't want it to be tough. If I were you I'd stuff it.'

'What will I stuff it with?'

'Pigs' said Mrs Buckland who was a resourceful and imaginative cook 'and then you would have some extra meat in case there wasn't enough to go round.'

Buckland worked for two days non-stop until he had finished the masterpiece of his later life 'How to cook an elephant.' Extracts of which now follow:

- Dig a pit 12 feet square and 8 feet deep (in the middle of Tom Quad)

- Construct tunnels at each corner to act as chimneys with a turn spit/bellows arrangement at each tunnel mouth

- Line bottom and sides with three feet of charcoal

- Light charcoal with small pastilles

- Insert prepared and oven-ready elephant

- Pour gravel and top soil over elephant to seal

- Keep fanning until the temperature reaches two hundred degrees Fahrenheit

- Cook for the required time and serve

In calculating the cooking time (thirty one and a half hours) Buckland took the bold decision to ignore heat losses through the earth, including the sides and ends of the pit. He reasoned that heat would be conducted through the meat and it would heat up until a state of equilibrium was reached, with as much heat being conducted through the meat as is lost to the earth, atmosphere etc. If the fire failed it might be possible that there would be insufficient heat to maintain the temperature of the meat at an adequate level but, he reasoned, some people may like their elephant rare. *Quod est demonstrandum* his feast would be ready on Thursday at 7.00pm.

Buckland, confident that his science would work, retired to bed.

'I'd like to see the look on Darwin's face when he hears about this,' he thought as sleep possessed him.

After morning prayers, Buckland with a supportive audience of Canons leaning from the windows of Tom Quad prepared for the mammoth task ahead of him. With the animal lying on her side he slowly paced across to the furthest wall of the quad, he turned and armed with a pikestaff ran like the clappers towards the beast. There was a loud pop, as the pike staff punctured Esmerelda's stomach and she started to deflate like a balloon. There was a hiss as her intestinal gases started to escape and moments later a torrent of blood sprayed out of the wound, covering Dr Buckland from head to toe.

'I was not expecting that,' he told his appreciative audience.

Esmerelda's now flaccid belly was supported by two of the strongest kitchen porters. Buckland, still dripping blood, slit her from front to back and then poked a small scullery boy into the opening with the injunction to hold his nose. The boy, who was known universally afterwards as Stinker, rummaged around inside the carcass throwing out the vital organs to Buckland's waiting arms.

To Buckland's satisfaction he managed to stretch her intestines all around the quad perimeter and passing students had to step daintily over them. A pack of fox hounds appeared and were keen to help. Their baying and howling, the gagging noises from Stinker as he emerged from the carcass, and the buzz of the thousands of bluebottles all contributed to the carnival atmosphere.

When Dr Buckland opened Esmerelda's stomach he was interested to find an inordinate quantity of half digested buns, one pound, seven and sixpence in small change and a bunch of keys. He made a mental note to return the keys to Mr Bostock. The college cooks stepped forward. Esmerelda was stuffed with three pigs, each pig stuffed with a capon and each capon stuffed with sweet bay leaves, and the cavity was sewn shut. Ropes were attached front and back.

Buckland arranged his work force into two teams. One team was to balance the animal while the other team was to move her into the pit or 'Elephantarium fornax' as it was now called. After much heaving the elephant was rolled into her final resting place.

Esmerelda was cooked lying on her back with her legs in the air and with the tip of her trunk sticking out of the oven to act as a pie-funnel.

The fire burnt, the elephant cooked, the smell of roasting meat filled Oxford. An interested crowd gathered at the gate to the quad and jostled to peer in. The dons stood around occasionally fanning the flames with their gowns. The undergraduates larked and the Very Reverend Buckland sharpened his carving knife.

As the bell, Big Tom, brother to the more famous Ben, struck seven, the pit was opened and the elephant was revealed. The cooks tied ropes around her legs and dragged her up onto the remnants of the lawns where they started to carve her.

In Christ Church's ancient dining hall the tables were laid for the feast. The college's silver and crystal glinted in the candlelight. The blue-faced gargoyles stuck their red tongues out rudely at the proceedings. The only woman at the feast was Elizabeth I who looked down from her portrait hung above the High Table. She would have enjoyed the event, having the stomach of a king. The doors opened and in staggered the college porters carrying trestle tables loaded with mountains of meat. The meat itself was a rather alarming red. At the lectern to the side of the top table Buckland stood to read the Horace-inspired epigram he had composed in place of the college's normal grace:

*Nunc est bibendum, nunc pede libero barrus pulsanda tellus.*

This translates as 'Now is the time for drinking, now is the time to beat the earth with unfettered elephants' feet'.

He sat down pleased with himself. His fellow masters all applauded politely and then started a critical debate as to what he should have said – barrus pulsanda or barrus pulsande. The argument still runs to this day.

Esmerelda fed three hundred people with enough leftovers to keep the workhouse in broth for a month. Buckland was the first to be served. He piled his plate high as an encouragement to the others. He selected for himself the animal's tail as a particular delicacy. Esmerelda's trunk, a little charred on the outside was carved into pretty rings, like calamari. He had one of those as well. Cumberland sauce was served as an accompaniment. He had thought long and hard as to what beverages should accompany the meal. In the stygian darkness of the college's wine cellar he had come across a box labelled 'Ritual Siberian Shaman Elixir.' This substance is made by Siberian shamans, who consume large quantities of the hallucinogenic fly agaric mushroom. The tribe wanting to share in the shaman's experience then drink his urine. These samples had been donated to the college in 1837 by Colonel FFyens Todgerington after his wife had mistakenly opened a bottle and given it to her bridge ladies.

'Just the thing' he said.

As the dark brown viscous liquid was poured into the masters' glasses the students looked quietly relieved that, through college funding cuts, they were limited to beer. It took the party nearly five hours to consume the meal.

And what did it taste like? It was agreed by most people that it was an acquired taste. Buckland thought it tasted like crocodile.

*Also published in Tell Tails edited by Wendy Greenberg*

୬ชเวิด୬

*Some of this story is true and the bits that aren't should be. Esmerelda's skeleton can be found in the Oxford University Museum of Natural History. Scorch marks from the fire are visible on the front and rear legs. Close examination of the left hand femur shows what looks like marks from the carving knife. St Giles Fair takes place on the Monday and Tuesday following the first Sunday after St Giles Day in September each year. Christ Church is open throughout the year. Tom Quad is the quad glimpsed from St Aldates. Esmerelda's pit is in the middle. DO NOT WALK ON THE GRASS.*

*The Very Reverend William Buckland, Canon of Christ Church and Dean of Westminster was born in 1784 and died in 1849. His rooms were in Corpus Christi College.*

# Passing Time

## *Kathleen Daly*

'Y ou're actually in very good shape for your age, Mrs Henderson. Perhaps you need a hobby to take your mind off things.'

Hetty glared at the doctor, who was already retreating behind her printer. Telling her what to do, indeed. How old was the girl? Twenty five? Thirty? They all looked younger than they were, nowadays. They never grew up.

'I'll just take that repeat prescription, thank you, doctor.'

You could never get a male doctor nowadays, either, only women part-timers. In her day, bringing up a family was a full-time job. There was no time for a career. You stayed single if you wanted that. She must make sure she didn't get this particular doctor, next time. She needed someone more mature. Her bones crunched as she rose, and, leaning on her stick, hobbled to the door.

She creaked her way from the surgery into Bury Knowle Park, stopping to catch her breath. The grey sky pressed down on the limp trees, threatening more rain. Under Hetty's gaze, a quaking terrier scurried back to its owner. As usual, she couldn't get that doctor's advice out of her head. The more she disagreed with something, the more it buzzed round in her head like a hungry wasp.

That doctor should know better. Hobbies, indeed. She realised she'd spoken aloud, and glanced furtively round the Headington supermarket. No one had heard her. The other shoppers were too busy rounding up their brawling offspring to pay her any attention. Then, defiantly, she muttered, 'I'll show her.'

She scowled at a toddler who was beating his fists against his mother's belly. While the woman was distracted, Hetty slipped past her to the check out, picking up the local papers on the way.

Back home, she sipped her tea, and ran one finger down the newspaper column. That was no good, she couldn't stand cats. And flowers were too fiddly. Ah now, this would do nicely. Local, too.

She spent the weekend choosing, washing and pressing the clothes she needed. They still fitted, though her hat could do with a bit of padding-out. Her hair was so much thinner, now.

On Monday morning, she rose while it was still dark, and made herself a good breakfast. She'd need it, the seasons were on the turn and the wind had a real edge to it. She put on her thick black wool coat, pinned on her hat, and was about to close the door when she realised she had left her stick behind. Funny, that. Usually she couldn't move without it.

The last leaves of autumn swirled down the road, with the wind in pursuit like a playful cat. Clouds scudded against the lightening sky. At the bus stop, she scrutinised the drooping faces, the bodies hunched against the wind. She flexed her own shoulders and felt blood pulsing through her body. She still had some life left in her. She even smiled at the bus driver as she told him her destination.

At the roundabout, the bus wove through London-bound traffic, and into Bayswater Road, with its line of corrugated houses. Just before the city thinned into semi-rural suburbs, the driver set her down by two slender fawn-pink brick pillars. She strode between them, along a drive of yellow-berried holly, frozen conifers and the stark branches of trees in winter mourning. Ahead of her, regimented standard roses saluted the slender white columns of a portico.

She joined a skein of figures migrating from the car park to the safe haven of the buildings. As they waited to go in, they sized each other up, like jurors about to go into court for the first time. A bagpipe pierced the air. The piper's knees were blue under his red kilt. Rather him than her. A voice beside her quavered, 'Are you a friend of his, dear?'

This could be awkward. She'd better keep it vague.

'We were good friends, but we lost touch years ago. I just saw the notice in the paper. Do you know him well?'

'I'm his sister, dear ...'

A playful gust spun the old biddy out of earshot. Hetty let herself fall back to the end of the line.

The interior was sparsely furnished with seats and people, so she could stay away from her neighbours without seeming rude. Plenty of flowers, the flowers outnumbered the congregation. And there was proper music. Nowadays they often had that pop. Everyone got up and sang thinly, trailing after the organ. Hetty could do better than that. She filled her lungs and bellowed tunefully. A frail gentleman at the far end of the row dropped his hymnbook. A child started to sob, and was hushed.

The vicar walked to the front, elegant in a coal-black cassock, snowy surplice and purple stole. A pity it was a woman, probably another part-timer. She settled down to enjoy the 'address', as they now called the sermon. Of course she knew he couldn't have been as good as they made him out to be. It would be a year or two before you'd hear an honest opinion. Still, it must be nice to be the centre of attention. Nice wood too, maple by the look of it, and stainless steel handles fine enough for a fitted kitchen. Such a shame to burn it.

The peach-blush and strawberry-crush curtains swished together. She took out a handkerchief and dabbed her eyes. This was real drama, an existence boiled down into ten minutes' commentary by a stranger. Much better than staying in and watching the rubbish on telly. She imagined herself telling that nice young doctor,

'Well, I've found a new hobby, my dear.'

Till death did her part, she decided, she would be the woman who went to funerals.

৯৪৩৫০৯

Bury Knowle Park surrounds a small mansion housing the public library; both were acquired in 1932 by Oxford City Council. The park has a ha-ha, a sensory garden, and a fine children's playground. It is a favourite with local dog-walkers. Bury Knowle Surgery adjoins the park, but does not boast Hetty among its patients!

Oxford Crematorium opened in 1939. It lies about three miles east of the City Centre, in the London direction. The extensive Garden of Remembrance is open to visitors. Buses run from St Aldate's, but services are not frequent. By car from the city centre, follow directions to the A40, along London Road, past Headington shops to Green Road roundabout, and take the second exit to Bayswater. You will find the Crematorium about half a mile further on.

# *Blind Date*

## *Wendy Greenberg*

Relaxation came easy at The Old Parsonage. Lucy eased herself into the soft armchair. The walls were Russian red and covered with eclectic portraits and cartoons.

The divorce had been taking its toll and she was at last ready to put Freddie behind her. Would she recognise her 'strong but soft' blind date? As she studied the menu and ordered the Very High Tea as they had arranged online, he walked in through the seventeenth century entrance porch.

'And you must be . . .'

Lucy glimpsed the red rose before his voice tailed off. She raised her eyes and they met Freddie's.

ഇൻഇൻ

*Enjoy the best afternoon tea at The Old Parsonage Hotel. The building dates back to Cromwell's time and is located in central Oxford between Keble and Somerville Colleges.*

# The Lily Pond

## *Kamini Khanduri*

As the bells of Magdalen tower chimed the quarter hour, Alice pushed the palm house door shut behind her. She slumped back against the glass and a wave of humidity hit her like a slap in the face. She inhaled deeply, half intoxicated by the exotic scents. Overhead, the clear Oxford skies were masked by a canopy of lush green foliage. It was hard to believe that the Botanic Garden was only metres away from the bustle of the High Street with its traffic and roadworks. But even in here, she couldn't escape. The voice of the man on the television came back to her: 'We will always remember her sparkling green eyes and her beautiful smile.' Beside him, his wife had sat motionless, her face drawn and grey, unable to look up at the flashing cameras. The grieving pair. The parents of the dead girl. Alice shook herself. She had to stop dwelling on it. After all, it might never have happened.

She wandered, lost in the tropical paradise. Her shoulders loosened and her mouth relaxed into a smile.

She began to feel peaceful. If there was anywhere she'd be able to forget, it would be here. She stroked the rough trunk of the cocoa tree and ran her fingers up and down the tall multi-sectioned stems of a sugar-cane plant. Perhaps she should tell someone. But what would she say? Nestling at the foot of the trees were clumps of red fly agaric mushrooms with their white-spotted tops. The label said that they had hallucinogenic properties. 'She was only seventeen,' the girl's father had said. Seventeen. Too young to die. How unfair that all these plants were thriving when the poor girl's life had been cut short. Alice's eyes prickled with tears. She stumbled past the cotton plant with its fluffy white balls and the rosy periwinkle, which, so the label said, produced chemicals that helped cure leukaemia. The blackbirds outside warbled and the leaves rustled soothingly, like a sigh, almost like a whisper . . . Was that a whisper? She looked round but no one was there. It must have been the ferns moving as she brushed past.

The path led to the lily pond. Out of breath, Alice rested against the rocky edge and watched the tadpoles and tiny fish darting in the murky water. Her stomach was churning and her hands were sticky with sweat. When she closed her eyes, she could see the girl's mother's accusing face.

Around the pond grew water lettuce, rice plants and papyrus. There were banana plants, their ridged leaves stretching up to the sun. And the lilies themselves – huge flat pads sitting on the pond's surface. Some smooth, some spiky, some small and some as large as dinner plates. 'Victoriana cruziana' Alice read on one label. With a perfect lip around its edge, it resembled an over-sized pie dish and was apparently strong enough to hold the weight of a child. The exquisite flowers were splashes of colour scattered around the pond. There were delicate white flowers, their partly-closed petals curving upwards into a point. Creamy yellow flowers like giant buttercups. And deep purple flowers with spiky pink-tipped petals and golden centres. The pineapple-sweet fragrance of the lilies filled Alice's nostrils. She began to feel hopeful. Everything would be all right.

And again, there was the whispering. She spun round. Was someone playing tricks? But no one was there.

'For God's sake Alice, get a grip. Now you're imagining things,' she muttered to herself as she moved away from the pond. *Alice* – it came again. She froze. It must be the leaves. Her heart was beating fast. It was too hot, she decided. She'd go and cool down in the alpine house. As she retraced her steps she couldn't help noticing that the path was made of hardened mud.

'That's strange,' she thought, 'I'm sure it used to be wooden decking? Anyway, the door's just round this next bend.' But it wasn't. The path meandered on, but no door appeared. And now she couldn't see any glass walls. Just thick foliage. No glasshouse roof, its panes crisscrossed with metal frames. Just the huge curving branches, and beyond them endless blue sky. A shiver ran down her spine and she felt panic. Where the hell was the exit? She started to hurry. *Alice! Alice!* It sounded closer now. The hairs on her arms were standing up. 'Who's there?' she called.

She began to run. 'Is anyone there?' she shouted. But no one answered. And now she was crying, her legs felt weak, her head was spinning. The strong scents of the tropical plants, which only a while ago had helped her relax, were now overpowering and unbearably sickly. She stumbled and fell, crawled under some branches and collapsed on the soil, leaning back against the comforting firmness of a gnarled tree trunk. Instead of the blackbird's song, she could hear parrots squawking, cicadas chirping, and monkeys chattering. The father's voice was ringing in her ears: 'Nothing will bring her back . . .We'd like to appeal to the driver . . .'

*She had been driving along the ring road, Elgar's cello concerto blasting from the CD player. It was midnight on a cool clear evening and the roads were empty. They'd just had the biggest row of their entire marriage. In the end, she'd snapped. Draining her glass of wine, she smashed it to the floor, watched it splinter into fragments and slammed out of the house. As she drove away, she opened her mouth and let out a deeply satisfying roar.*

Now in the glasshouse, it seemed to be getting dark and the heat was stifling. The sound of the monkeys was louder and she could hear something large moving through the foliage. She swallowed with fear. Her mouth was full of saliva but her throat was dry. 'Water!' she gasped. 'I need water.'

*She knew she was breaking the speed limit, but who was there to see? A group of people was crossing the road ahead. They were some distance away and without needing to touch the brake, she watched them safely reach the opposite side. She congratulated herself on her sound judgement despite having had a few drinks.*

Staggering to her feet, she followed the path until she found herself back at the lily pond. Relieved to see a familiar landmark, she sank to her knees at the pond's edge and dipped her hands in the water. Tepid rather than cold, it was still refreshing and she plunged her arms in up to the elbows.

*The music soared as it reached a climax. She sang along and put her foot down, enjoying her control of the vehicle. Then a shape appeared as if from nowhere. A shape in the road, moving from side to side. Was it a person? Was she just imagining it?*

Alice lifted her arms from the water and breathed slowly, trying to calm herself. 'A girl of seventeen has been killed by a hit-and-run driver,' the newscaster had said. Alice pressed her hands over her ears. Her face was burning hot.

*Feeling confused, she slammed on the brake. The car started to slow but it was too late. There was a dull thud as she hit something. A person? Or just a branch from an overhanging tree. Or maybe an animal – a fox or a deer? She'd been driving too fast. And she'd had too much to drink.*

Leaning over the pond, she closed her eyes and splashed the soothing water onto her cheeks. And then it came again. *Alice. Alice.* But this time it was different. More like a gurgle than a whisper or a sigh. As if it was underwater. Frozen with fear, Alice opened her eyes. And there, centimetres away from her, just under the surface of the water, was a face. The face of a young girl with green eyes.

やめ**80C3**めや

*Take a stroll up High Street to find a few moments of peace in a busy city. Beyond Queen's Lane but just before Magdalen Bridge you'll find Oxford's Botanic Garden. The garden was founded in 1621 on the banks of the River Cherwell in the corner of Christ Church Meadow. It stands on land that was once a Jewish cemetery. It's the oldest botanic garden in Britain, one of the oldest scientific gardens in the world, and is home to 7,000 different types of plant – though they're not all on display. There's more biological diversity here than there is in a tropical rainforest! Visit the glasshouses and marvel at the giant lilies in the Lily House, search for cocoa, oranges, pawpaws and coconuts in the tropical Palm House, or escape to the desert in the Cactus House. Then wander in the walled garden and have a look for the oldest tree – the English yew planted by the garden's first curator, Jacob Bobart, in 1645. Can you find the black pine tree, now one of the largest trees in the garden? This tree has been the inspiration for many writers, from J. R. R. Tolkien to Philip Pullman. And Lewis Carroll, the Oxford mathematics professor who wrote Alice's Adventures in Wonderland, was a frequent visitor in the 1860s. In fact, you can see the dome of the Lily House in the background of one of Tenniel's classic illustrations for Carroll's book.*

# *Just Another Tuesday*

## *Andrew Bax*

As Joyce waited for the bus there was nothing to warn her that this Tuesday would be different. Off and on for nearly 60 years, she and Mildred had met for elevenses and always on a Tuesday. It was a routine that suited them both; apart from that and a shared interest in needlework, they had little in common. They had been friends at school and when they went their separate ways prim, beautiful Mildred, groomed for marriage by her ambitious parents, was sent to finishing school. On her return she promptly fell for an austere young man of lofty intellect who eventually became Wilsonian Professor of Byzantine Art at Pembroke College. Dumpy little Joyce had become a clerical assistant for the council and married into trade. Her husband was a butcher and they lived above the shop in Walton Street. She had only moved after his recent death and because of the surprising discovery that she had become the owner of five houses and three race horses. Yesterday, one of them had come in at five to one at Pontefract and she was bursting to tell Mildred about it.

Mildred, meanwhile, was waiting, wearily, for the bus at Rose Hill. The long walk from her retirement home, The Firs, had made her stiff. The Firs was a place of meagre comforts but it was all she could afford. She envied Joyce her four-room Abingdon Road apartment with a bus stop right outside, a live-in warden and an indoor swimming pool. When Mildred had heard about the swimming pool, envy had made her say crossly 'I've never heard anything so ridiculous. Who wants to swim at our time of life?' But she mustn't get cross she reminded herself. Although it was a struggle to get into town, she looked forward to these Tuesday meetings; they broke up the week and Joyce was a good listener. And this week, she had something exciting to tell her.

Joyce was the first to get to the Queen's Lane Coffee House and secured their usual table near the Ladies. Why hadn't Jimmy told her about the horses, she wondered. She knew he liked a little flutter – and why not? But then, they had never been short of money and she had always left that side of things to Jimmy. He was the business man after all and when he passed on – bless him – he left her very well provided for.

So when the trainer rang, the previous week, to suggest Joyce put a little bet on Port Meadow she had no hesitation in agreeing to £200. And she made a profit of £1000 – just like that!

Just then the door opened and Mildred weaved her way between the tables. Joyce smiled a welcome.

'You look happy' Mildred said.

'I am. And I'll tell you why.'

As Mildred listened to the Pontefract story she reflected on what she would do with £1000. It seemed a huge amount of money to her. She needed a new pair of shoes for a start. And it would be nice to go on a cruise. Somewhere exotic, like the Caribbean. Yes, the Caribbean would be nice. And then what about the children – and the grandchildren and, goodness, the great grandchildren! Suddenly £1000 didn't seem a lot of money after all. What would Joyce do with it, she wondered. Probably give it to the first Big Issue seller she saw. Mildred sighed.

'So I'm paying for elevenses today,' Joyce was saying. From the very beginning they had each paid their share because Mildred always had something rather plain, like shortbread, but Joyce could never resist a rich and creamy cake, which cost more.

'Joyce' she laughed 'There's no need for that.'

'Go on, let me pay just this once,' Joyce insisted.

Mildred sighed then smiled. 'All right, I'll celebrate your win with a little . . .' she looked at the display cabinet '. . . with a little carrot cake. And I have some exciting news about Edwin' she added.

Joyce settled herself for another long story about Mildred's talented family. Five children: they came popping out as regular as clockwork until Mildred began to look quite exhausted, poor dear. And as for Alexander – well! Thin as a stick and no conversation. Just shows you never know what goes on behind closed doors.

As Mildred recounted Edwin's life history, one she

had told many times before, Joyce tried to remember who he was. One of the younger grandsons, she concluded, the one whose parents weren't married. Mildred had been terribly upset about them 'living in sin' until Edwin was born. Now they could do nothing wrong.

'And now,' Mildred announced, 'he's been offered a place at Brookes.'

'That's nice, dear,' said Joyce 'What will he be doing there?'

'Media studies' replied Mildred. She hoped Joyce wouldn't ask her what that meant because she didn't know herself.

'That sounds awfully modern.'

'It is. And Brookes has one of the best courses in the country. Hundreds of candidates apply, but they only take the cream.' Mildred knew she sounded smug but couldn't help it. 'And lots of good jobs afterwards,' she added. Whatever it was, she was certain there were better prospects in media studies than in Byzantine art. Sometimes she felt a little bitter about the hand that fate had dealt her. Alexander had been so wrapped up in his work, writing books that nobody read, and poking about in dirty old monasteries, that he seemed to forget about her for weeks on end. But at least she had the family.

'Such a shame you didn't have children, Joyce,' Mildred sighed, and not for the first time. And, as usual, Joyce replied, 'But you've made up for both of us.' In fact, Joyce's only regret was that she and Jimmy didn't have children. He would have been a good dad, and with all the money he had been making, he would have given them a good start in life. Still, she smiled to herself, they had fun trying.

Theirs had been a marriage of harmonious contentment in which, as time passed, their separate lives merged into one. People were surprised at how well Joyce had adapted to being alone but in the dark, silent hours, she was grieving deeply. All she wanted was to join her Jimmy.

Now Mildred was talking about Jeremy. Was he the one in the BBC, or was that Rupert? Joyce tried to look interested but a sort of sizzling sound made it difficult to concentrate. More of a bubbling than a sizzling she decided, and leant forward to hear what Mildred was saying.

'. . . and do you know what? They said he couldn't come back unless . . .'

Joyce suddenly felt very, very tired. The bubbling had turned into a kind of popping. She closed her eyes.

'. . . they had to agree to that, of course . . .' The pops were getting louder. And then there was no sound at all.

'Joyce! Joyce – are you all right?' No reply. 'Joyce!' Mildred almost shouted.

She gave Joyce's leg a little kick under the table. No response. She kicked again, harder this time. Nothing.

Shocked, frightened and confused, Mildred stared at her old friend, now leaning gently against the table, apparently asleep. Then, in a daze, she got up, waved vaguely to the waitress, and went home.

And Joyce went to join her Jimmy.

৯৪৪৪৩৫৬

*The Queen's Lane Coffee House is an excellent venue for snacks and light meals. There has been an Oxford eatery on this site for as long as anyone can remember – just next to the Palladian extravagance of The Queen's College at the lower end of High Street, where it is at its widest. All the buses to and from Marston, Headington, Cowley and Rose Hill stop here – and the X13 from the Abingdon Road on its way to the John Radcliffe Hospital, which is the bus Joyce would have caught for her Tuesday elevenses with Mildred.*

# Gargoyles

## S. A. Edwards

The gargoyles that infested the buildings of Oxford were spreading, peering down from the roof tops and pulling faces. But they were the old ones. Too old to do her any harm. Their powers eroded.

But now new young ones had started creeping limpet-like down the buildings and were peeping into windows, watching her. They had started breeding, adapting and changing.

What would they do when they reached the ground? They wouldn't need to live on buildings any more.

She had seen them pretending to be ornaments, for God's sake, selling themselves in the tourist shops. They'd stuck themselves on to postcards. Is that how they were spreading? They were clever – she'd give them that.

Sitting in Café Loco on St Aldates, she ordered a coffee. The pretty Polish girl put it on the table.

'Are you OK? Is there a problem?' the girl asked gently.

She shook her head not lifting her eyes.

She knew there was one close, one low down, but she couldn't see it. When the waitress had gone she looked carefully around. She examined the ceiling, no gargoyles. Perhaps she was imagining it. Maybe it was just the gargoyles from Christ Church, the licheny bastards.

Then she saw it, pretending to be graffiti, spray painted on to a grey telecom box opposite the café window and low down almost at pavement level.

It caught her eye then looked away.

So that was their game.

৯৹৪৩৫৵

*Café Loco, The Old Palace, St Aldates. The café is located in a Grade 1 sixteenth-century building. Graffiti on the telecom box located on Rose Street opposite the café windows may be by the elusive artist Banksy or may be worthless graffiti. You decide.*

# *Weighing it All Up*

## *Wendy Greenberg*

Slow autumn light stumbled through the curtains, across Stella's sleepless pallor, signalling decision time. Should she stay or should she go? Through the tenebrous hours she had been weighing up her options. She turned into the magnet of Eddie's warmth, observing with astonishment his breath rising and falling, sleep enveloping every familiar feature, whilst she lay shrouded in her regular insomnia. She laid her hand across his back and indulged in a few carefree moments beside him, before she began today's leap of faith.

She had met Charles in the bike shop. He had come with his team to persuade the owner to stock their new brand in the flagship St Michael's Street shop. By the time the bikes were in stock, Charles had insinuated himself into Stella's life. She had not been looking for love, but after that first heady evening together she had not been hard to reel in. They fell into an easy habit with one another, and the year had begun to slip away when he startled her.

'When I'm with you, Stella, my life feels complete, stay with me, come and live with me.' He had reached for her, gently covering her hand and brushing it with his lips, 'I love you,' and as he pulled her close and held her tightly, she whispered, realising, that it was true, 'And I love you too Charles.'

She adored this striking man with the velvet voice. She was spellbound by his words. But all along there had been Eddie. Handsome, loyal, gorgeous Eddie, who always stood by her. How could she choose?

Charles knew about Eddie, and despite the living arrangements, did not consider him a serious rival, but Eddie can only have guessed about Charles from Stella's long absences. When Stella was home he silently inveigled himself into her affection with ease. He wriggled into Stella's arms and she stroked his head, embracing him as if nothing could possibly change their close bond.

Stella pulled back the bedclothes, preparing to rise, and Eddie stirred. She swallowed and sighed. The maelstrom in the pit of her stomach raged as she picked up the phone beside the bed. Eddie was suddenly very awake, his sage coloured eyes expectant. She replaced the receiver.

'Eddie ...I have to talk to you.'

They looked at each other for a moment and Stella's heart melted. She couldn't leave Eddie, what had she been thinking? She would have to break it off with Charles. She got out of bed, and with the relief of having made a decision, smiled at Eddie. He wrapped himself around her legs, purring as his tail caressed her. He had no regrets. If sensitivity to cats was a deal breaker for Charles, so be it – after all, faint heart never won fair lady!

*Also published in* Tell Tails *edited by Wendy Greenberg*

࿇ ❧

*Bike Zone (28–32 St Michael's Street) is part of the old city north wall boundary. According to the 1939 survey of the City, 'The section of wall between New Inn Hall Street, where there was a postern, and Cornmarket Street is now reduced to a length on the north side of 24 St Michael's Street. A short distance east of the postern there was a bastion, now destroyed. The surviving length of wall is probably medieval at the base but the upper part has been reconstructed.'*

*The North Gate through the wall placed at the east end of St Michael's Street spanned Cornmarket Street to St Michael-at-the-Northgate Church. It was pulled down in 1771.*

*Today you can see the remains of no. 2 bastion (13th century) at the rear of 28–32 St Michael's Street. The buildings on the north side of St Michael's Street would have been built up against and merged with the thick city wall. The site is not only a relic of the city's ancient defences but equally has experienced many events of Oxford's history such as the Great Fire in 1644 which damaged a significant amount of St Michael's Street.*

*St Michael's Street itself has also had many names. In 1405, it was Wood Street; in 1548, Bocardo Lane (named after the prison at the North Gate); in 1751 New Inn Hall Street making it a T-shaped road until 1899 when it came to own the name St Michael's Street.*

# *In Memory of Comets*

## *Janet Bolam*

'Mum, is Joe eating with us tonight?' 'Yes, and before you find an excuse not to be there, remember the pocket money deal.'

Susan watched her daughter as she debated between sharing a meal with Joe and the prospect of enough money to buy a pretty top she'd seen. It was worth one more try.

'But I feel sick and I'll puke up all over the table if I have to watch him eating, I know I will.' Susan settled her eye on her 13 year old daughter and thrust some plates into her hand. 'Set the table and shut up.' Every week it was the same. Joe had started to come to dinner once a week in the early post operative days when he found it difficult to adjust to life with one leg. Now he was managing very well, but the habit of the weekly meal was firmly established in his mind, so every Monday he would call to confirm that he was expected and every week Susan and Mandy argued about it.

It was generally acknowledged that Joe was amazing for his age. Even though he only had one leg, he refused a wheelchair, preferring to walk with a false leg. He lived alone in his own ground floor flat. There was little that did not interest him. His visits were peppered with eager questions and debate on topics as varied as the politics of the day (too right wing), the latest play at the Playhouse (he preferred the classics), and his beloved music. He still played his violin in a small quartet and after dinner he would frequently play the piano for the family, loosely banging out chords, singing Gershwin and Sondheim, much to Mandy's distress.

His taxi drew up into the drive.

Davy viewed 'Joe evenings' with great delight. It was Davy who first called him Gungy Joe. This referred to the drifts of dandruff mixed liberally with clippings from his beard that permanently coated his shoulders and rolled down his food-stained shirt.

'So kind, so kind.' Joe wobbled his way into the living room. He was still a little unstable, tending to stop and sway dramatically at regular intervals. ' I've brought you a present. Some homemade yoghurt with garlic.' He indicated a grubby plastic bag tied onto his stick. Susan carefully extracted it and helped Joe to a seat.

'Mandy loves your homemade yoghurt.' With an evil leer Davy took the grey leaking jar from the bag and waved it in front of his sister's face. Mandy, who had been trying not to breathe through her nose since Joe's arrival managed a smile.

'How nice and thoughtful of you Joe.' Susan took the

jar away into the kitchen followed closely by Mandy

'Mum' she whispered urgently 'He absolutely stinks.'

'Yes, it does seem a bit worse than usual,' Susan agreed.

'A bit! I can't bear it. You're not putting that stuff into the fridge are you?'

'Just until he goes home. A mark of respect.'

Conversation around the table was lively. Davy was learning about comets at school and it had caught his imagination. This was no surprise since the comet Hale Bopp had been making spectacular appearances in the night sky for the past 3 months.

'Isn't that the one that was discovered by Halley?' ventured Susan.

'Oh Mum! That's Halley's comet, not Hale-Bopp. I can't believe you thought that!' Sometimes Mandy found lesser mortals trying, especially her mother.

'I remember my mother told me she saw Halley's comet when she was a girl. There were no electric street lights in those days, so it could be seen very clearly. She told me that she agreed to marry my father the day she saw it. Fireworks.' Joe pierced a pea that flew to the ground to join the rest of the food scattered around his feet.

'Halley's comet came in 1910 then 1986 and it's going to come again in 2061.' Davy was a mine of information. 'When we go on our school trip, we're going to see the house he lived in. There's an Observatory on the top. Halley was the one who discovered that it was the same one coming back and back and back. . . .'

'What school trip?' Susan realised she had not mined Davy's school bag for notes from school for quite some time.

'The one I've been telling you about. I bet you don't know the difference between a comet and an asteroid, Mandy.'

'Why would I care?' Mandy was edging towards the door.

'Comets have tails and asteroids don't! What do you think the tail is made of?'

'I read an advertisement for plane rides.' Joe helped himself to more potatoes. 'You can hire them at Kidlington Airport and they take you up at night so that you can see the comet clearly. We would be above all the electric lights and see it just like my mother and father did.'

'But it's not the same comet . . .' Mandy started, but caught Susan's eye and held her tongue.

'Yes, it would be magical to do that.' Joe blinked behind his glasses. 'Wonderful potatoes, Susan. I don't suppose I could interest any of you in a plane ride?'

The small plane sat on the airfield, the engine running. Joe slowly crossed the tarmac with Susan anxiously holding his elbow to prevent him falling. Davy was already mounting the steps onto the plane. He could hardly contain himself. 'Can I sit next to the pilot? Do you think we will see the edge of the Milky Way? Will we be able to see the Comet's tail?' At 4000 feet above

Oxfordshire, the plane turned north. The Pilot could be heard over the headphones.

'A good night for comet watching,' he was saying. 'We will soon see Banbury.'

'You look very pale darling,' Susan noticed her daughter was clutching her middle. 'Are you OK?'

'I feel sick.' She leaned forward, grabbed a paper bag and retched. Meanwhile Joe, who had been staring intently out of his window, let out a long, low fart. Mandy vomited.

'This is the best view I have ever seen of the comet!' The pilot continued unaware of the visceral drama being enacted in the passenger compartment. 'Those of you on the left-hand side can see it now.'

Craning her neck, Susan stared hopefully into the heavens. Joe had his handkerchief out and was alternating attempts to clean the window with bashing his glasses as he pushed his head next to the thick glass. The stars were bright pinpoints on a black velvet sky. 'Do you think that's the comet?' Susan and Mandy stared doubtfully at Venus. 'No, but aren't the stars amazing? Even if we don't see the comet, it's worth it.'

Mandy smiled.

'Beautiful clarity tonight' the pilot said. 'One more time around and then we must prepare for landing.'

Joe banged his walking stick on the glass furiously. The comet appeared to be hovering right outside his window, like a visiting Greek god. Surreal, large and bright with its tail divided into two fins, it was perfectly framed by the window.

They watched, transfixed until the plane turned and it disappeared from view.

On the way home in the taxi, Davy slept between Susan and Mandy. Joe sat in the front seat, smiling as he remembered his Mother's face, animated as she described the incredible day she saw Halley's comet.

*In memory of Fred Porter, who was a dear friend.*

❧❧❧❧

*Edmund Halley (1656–1742) was an English astronomer and mathematician who was the first to calculate the orbit of the comet later named after him. While in Oxford, he attended The Queen's College and lived in a modest white house, near the Bridge of Sighs on New College Lane, which also accommodated his Observatory. A plaque, just visible through the bushes, marks the spot. The range of Halley's scientific interests was enormous: he did work on the variation of the earth's magnetic field, the variation of barometric pressure with height, the salinity and evaporation of oceans, and the optics of the rainbow. He also translated the geometrical works of Apollonius and even reconstructed a missing section. Without him, Newton's Principia would not have existed, for it was Halley who pressed Newton to publish and who paid for the printing himself.*

*In 1703 Halley was elected to the Savilian Chair of Geometry at Oxford and ended his career as Astronomer Royal. He died in 1742 after drinking a glass of wine against his doctor's orders. He was eighty-six.*

# *An Unhistorical Act*

## *Jackie Vickers*

Candida lived in the closest and most affectionate of all possible families, yet she still felt there was something missing.

'What is the meaning of life?' Candida asked Mona Lisa, her cat, whose impassive expression gave nothing away. 'Why are we here?' she asked her reflection in the mirror. She even asked her parents.

'If you want an answer to that sort of question, you had better study philosophy,' said her father, who believed education was the answer to everything.

Her favourite occupation was cooking and as her parents and sisters were generally disorganised and perpetually hungry, they encouraged this interest.

'You're so good at it,' said one of her sisters.

'And it benefits us all,' agreed another.

'It allows the rest of us to "peruse the greater mysteries",' said a third, who was reading Sir Thomas

Browne, and liked everyone to know it.

But no-one offered any answer to Candida's question, in spite of all the time they spent reading.

'Maybe they read the wrong books,' Candida whispered to Mona Lisa.

So she set off one sunny spring morning, when all North Oxford gardens were bursting with pink and white blossom, determined to answer her own question. She was confident she would answer it in a matter of weeks.

The Natural History Museum, with its cast-iron roof trusses and imposing façade, seemed a good place to start. The swifts were wheeling and screaming around the tower, which had housed generations of these birds for the last sixty years. In the display cabinets on the upper gallery were live cockroaches, and tarantulas, which made Candida squeamish. She read the detailed descriptions by every display but even the stick insects seemed inscrutable. She felt cross.

'What is the point of a stick insect?' she asked a thin young man with glasses, who was taking notes.

'That's a silly question,' he said without looking at her.

'That is the most important question about a stick insect,' she retorted.

She spent longer with the bees, who were more satisfying. Their glass sided structure hung from the landing window, so that visitors could observe them. While she found bee life too complex to absorb in just one visit, Candida did grasp that, with no opportunity for a career change, it clearly mattered whether you were a drone or a worker.

'Not much free-will here,' she remarked to a young mother who held a wriggling, squealing child.

'Nor anywhere else!' was the tart reply.

As Candida cycled home through the park she reflected that apart from the bees and the visiting swifts, the museum collection of stuffed birds and animals said more about death than life. It was certainly more about how things lived and died than about why they did, so she decided to look elsewhere for enlightenment.

The following morning Candida decided to visit the Bodleian Library. 'It holds one of the world's greatest collections,' she said, hitching up her biggest rucksack, which would carry at least a dozen books.

'But . . .' began her parents.

Candida did not wait to hear their objections.

She had never been inside, so the elaborate ceiling of the Divinity school took her by surprise. An elderly man who was rubbing the back of his neck smiled at her.

'I get a crick in my neck every time I come here!'

'It's amazing,' said Candida, wishing she could say something more intelligent.

'Perpendicular, excellent example of lierne vaulting. Look at the bosses,' he added.

She flipped through a pamphlet telling of the acquisitions, donations, collections, and the changing functions of the different buildings in different centuries.

Visitors were gathering to take the next guided tour of the building, but she decided instead to make some attempt on the eight million books currently held there. She liked the sound of Duke Humfrey's library and the Upper Reading Room.

A porter asked to see her ticket and laughed when she explained that she had purposely brought her biggest bag.

'This isn't a lending library! They even refused to let the King borrow a book.'

'Which King?'

'King Charles the First, the one who was executed.'

'They have had nearly four hundred and fifty years to change the rules!' she said.

'And only members of the University and visiting academics have the right to a Bodleian ticket,' the porter added.

Later that evening Candida hugged her cat for comfort, and decided it was lonely trying to solve one of life's great mysteries. She took down the Yellow Pages, flipped through it and discovered there were seventy entries under 'places of worship'. Perhaps there she would find the meaning of life by learning about the different religions and sects.

In the Oxford library, the librarian sat Candida in front of a computer and left her to read Wikipedia's extensive entry. An hour later she was still reading.

'There are so many different opinions,' she said

helplessly. 'I've read the outlines of all the leading philosophies but I haven't even started on religion.'

'It's a big subject. Maybe too big to come to any final decision just yet. Have you seen this?' the librarian asked, giving her an Art Weeks booklet. 'You may find meaning in Art.'

That year there were over four hundred entries from all the professionals, amateurs, art groups and even schools, scattered all over Oxfordshire. Within the city boundary, there were one hundred and sixty studios and exhibition spaces open to the public that week. Candida, who always tried to do things thoroughly, visited more than she could count, and returned every evening with her head spinning. She had looked at oils, watercolours and prints, at hand-woven and hand-dyed fabrics, at stained glass and jewellery. She had looked at pots: earthenware, stoneware and porcelain, coil pots, slab pots and hand thrown pots, fired in conventional kilns and wood-fired kilns, decorated and glazed in every conceivable colour and pattern.

On the last day of Art Weeks she spent her birthday money on a very large piece of pottery.

That evening Candida unwrapped her Art Week dish and put it on the kitchen table. Then she weighed out risotto rice and warmed it in a pan over low heat. At intervals one or other of her sisters would appear and ask what she was preparing for supper. She would laugh at their greedy expressions.

'Don't forget the mushrooms!' said her eldest sister.

'And there must be lots and lots of parmesan,' said

the youngest, doing a little tap-dance.

Then the twins came, saying they hoped Candida was making enough because the smell was wonderful, and they were very, very, hungry.

Finally her mother put her head round the door and shoo-ed them all away.

Left to herself once more, Candida felt a familiar uncertainty wash over her. But as she tasted the rice and hesitated over the seasoning, she realised that the most satisfying moments of the last few weeks had been spent in this kitchen making these small decisions. Candida massaged the creamy starch out of the rice, allowing each ladleful to be absorbed before adding the next. As she stirred, she thought for a moment about George Eliot's address to her readers, at the very end of *Middlemarch,* that the 'growing good of the world is partly dependent on unhistorical acts'. Candida removed the pan from the heat and slowly stirred in the mushrooms, butter, cream and parmesan, breathing in the rich aroma. I'll let others look for meaning, she decided as she filled the Art Week bowl with the risotto.

She put it on the table, and started to explain how 'unhistorical acts' can in themselves be meaningful.

But no-one was listening.

ଔ୧ଔଔଔ

*The Oxford University Museum of Natural History in Park Road houses the University's scientific collections of zoological, entomological and geological specimens. This Neo-Gothic building was completed in 1860 to accommodate the university science departments. Among its most famous features are the*

*Oxfordshire dinosaurs, the dodo, and the swifts in the tower. It is open daily and admission is free. The Bodleian Library is the Library of the University of Oxford and is one of the oldest and most important non-lending reference libraries in Britain. The Bodleian is particularly rich in Asian manuscripts and collections of English literature, local history, and early printing. Though it was established earlier, it was not secured by the university until 1410. After a period of decline, it was restored by Sir Thomas Bodley (1545–1613), a collector of medieval manuscripts, and reopened in 1602 when it was opened to scholars. Guided tours take place several times a day.*

*'Art Weeks' was established 25 years ago. For three weeks in May, around 400 artists and craftsmen open their Oxfordshire studios and homes to the public. There are also exhibitions in larger public spaces. Entry is free.*

# *Manuscript*

## *Kathleen Daly*

Welcome to my world. Perhaps you have come half-way across the globe to see me. Perhaps you have come across the street. I have been entombed in my box in the dim recesses of the library stacks. I have been waiting for you.

What will I be to you? You brush past the custodian, you seize me with a curt nod, you deposit me on the desk, rifle my contents, discard me. I shall be a mere footnote in your learned tome.

You, though, you enter silently, awed by the vacant spaces. Your eyes glide over the painted page of the ceiling to the splintered colours of the Selden End. You spy out the carols where so many eminent scholars have worked. You watch the Librarian unlock the wooden fortress enclosing Bodley's most precious manuscripts. You cradle me in your arms, you pose me on the foam lectern. You caress my crimson binding. You stroke the smooth flesh of my ivory leaves, the fine black follicles from corpses that went to create me. You devour my fluid script, the yellow flush of my majuscules, you savour the azure, the mallow, the burnished gold of my initials, the breast of a letter where a bee sits, its folded wings filmy and transparent. I am the key to your work, the evidence you have been searching for all your life, your illumination.

Feast on my intricate borders of lapis, scarlet, viridian. Birds swoop through ivy and acanthus leaves, dive among violets, strawberries and columbines. A cat claws their plumage. A monkey plays a pipe and tabor. Urns overflow with flowers. A monk bestrides a hobby horse. A child snares a rabbit in his hood.

Move beyond the frame. Glance through the open windows, at my landscapes. A peasant and his donkey cross the fields. A boat with its angler floats along a river, a watermill churns the current. Swans glide over a mirror lake. A shepherd herds sheep, while his wife gently guides them into a wattle pen. Knights ride towards the turrets of distant castles. City walls melt into a blue haze. Ships unfurl their sails on faraway seas. Rays of sun stream down from heaven like a benediction.

Look again at the foreground. Armies are locked in combat, death contorts the bodies of men and horses. This is the land of the Apocalypse, of war, famine, sickness, and death. Brothers turn against fathers. Invaders sweep across France. Cities are starved and looted, the countryside is laid waste. Inside my pages, my creators wage war.

My artist learned his trade in enemy territory. He was a collaborator's apprentice. While his Master painted the foreground of a scene, he drew the landscapes. How he yearns for those days, as his eyes turn to glass and his apprentices snigger at the old-fashioned images they copy from his pattern books.

My author is a patriot, whose book must be fit for the king he followed into exile. He orders my artist to paint the major figures, he doesn't want an apprentice foisted on him. He pays for the best pigments. But pictures themselves have no beauty or meaning. Only words count.

My artist hates my author, that tormentor, that clanging cymbal, though he cannot afford to turn away his business. My craftsman sees each picture as a web of illusion, of shape and pattern, light and shade, space and volume, where colours collide and separate, oppose and complement each other.

Reach into the picture. Feel the texture of velvet and silk and fine wool under your hand, the cold glaze of tiles under your feet. Step into this image. Watch blood vibrating in veins, spilling from wounds, hear laughter and cries of anguish. Inhale breath scented with cinnamon and cloves, the smoke of burning buildings, the odour of decay. Follow the path winding across the landscape. Run your hand up the bark of the tree. Grasp at the leather suspended over your head. Listen to the rope creaking in the breeze.

And when you have done shuddering, when you have run back the way you have come, scattering the sheep, astonishing the shepherd, when the knights have parted before your headlong flight, stretch out your hands and claw at the picture plane. Thrust back your chair. Rush from the library. Who will see your empty eyes? Who will notice one more figure in the landscape? The last scholar miscounted, it happens to the best of them. And I shall wait for my next reader.

ᏽᎧᏸᏣᏸᏍ

*Duke Humfrey's Library was constructed in the late fifteenth and seventeenth centuries and is part of the Old Bodleian Library (between Broad Street and Radcliffe Square). This story was inspired by the 'Historical Mirror of France' (MS Bodley 968) made in France at the end of the Hundred Years War (c.1451), and its fifteen fine illustrations. The manuscript is not on public display but there are regular guided tours of the Bodleian Library that include a visit to Duke Humfrey's Library. The rest is fiction: to the author's knowledge, no book in the Bodleian has ever devoured its reader.*

# *Love Me Do*

## *Wendy Greenberg*

Jodie, an atheist, had been brought to this sanctified spot by both serendipity and despair. She stood by the small prayer board in Magdalen College chapel reading the handwritten notices pinned there.

'Please pray for those whose names are written here. Please date your request'

> *Please pray for those who are lost like me, may I find my soul mate*
> *Please pray that that he is the right one for me*
> *Please pray that God will intervene and give me a husband. . .*

It seemed that the ubiquity of the quest for love was one area that united both town and gown.

She had fled from her house that morning after a bruising attempt to create an online dating profile with her friend Tess. Jodie's initial enthusiasm for the task had been quickly tempered after scanning through a host of registered users, trying to get a feel for how to market herself.

'Open Arms' called out with – just the best hugger and kisser.

'Tattoo Man' banged his drum with – I'm waiting for you.

'Fil_ander' was . . . surprise, surprise after sensual adventures.

'Master and Commander' was ready to take charge!

Jodie shuddered, in disbelief at the depths to which she had sunk to avoid another car-crash relationship. Now she was well out of her comfort zone in these sacred surroundings but she had not felt at ease in front of her monitor either. The infinite possibilities of the bulging dating sites felt a million miles away.

The chapel was deserted and a sense of peace descended on her. She adjusted to the subdued light and stepped across the large marble flagstones, imbibing the unfamiliar smell of tradition and establishment. The high vaulted ceiling and the colossal sepia-toned stained glass windows gave her a momentary sense of space. She edged away from the door and sank into the dark seating which curved up to her shoulders, holding her in its wooden embrace. She stroked the smooth wood, heavy with the scent of beeswax, put her head in her hands and felt choked by tears again. She yearned for that certain someone to share her life but fishing on a website had felt degrading, Tess was probably right.

The online dating had all started well enough.

'How would you describe me Tess?'

'I would describe you as my adorable, impetuous, reliable but maverick friend who loves life and has made a lot of poor choices – but I am not sure that is what is required here.'

'We'll gloss over that . . . User name first – Out to lunch? Gone to seed? Last Chance Saloon?'

'No, No, Jodie, I think you may have to take a more positive approach . . . what about Stardust? . . .'

'Nah! Too hippy dippy . . .'

'Golden Girl?'

'Jesus, Tess, don't you remember that sit-com about those retired women called the Golden Girls? . . . What about something like Beating Heart (not dead yet), Open Book (the plot unfolds), or Sassy Girl (ready to snap up)?'

The cracked old board hanging beside the chapel door was covered with a confetti-like collection of small white notices, each sheet cut uniformly, each handwritten notice arranged with geometric precision. A pile of empty paper lay in wait on the table ready to pounce on the hopes and fears of this academic community. Jodie gathered up a couple of the empty white sheets and settled back into the musty atmosphere, chewing the end of her pen thoughtfully.

Jodie began to write. She felt hypocritical and out of place in these surreal surroundings but there did not seem to be anything to lose in using this spiritual forum and its congregation to help her along her way.

Her arrival in the college had been unplanned;

rushing out after her row with Tess, she had slipped through the entrance to avoid another confrontation with her ex-brother-in-law who she had spotted on the High Street. The elderly college retainer casually took her entrance money, raised his eyes from the racing pages and directed her out into the quadrangle. Inside, her sore eyes widened, it was breathtaking, the old cobbles, the honey stonework, manicured lawn and the opulent wisteria twisting and climbing from perfectly dug beds to delicately fringe the mullioned windows with clusters of pale mauve petals. She followed the path to her right and joined the shady southern cloisters. It led her into the chapel through a doorway beneath the muniment tower.

In here, time stood still, the air felt weighty, distant whisperings of traffic and college activity barely registering. White petals fell onto the memorial stones from a carefully arranged display. She could not keep running from her demons. She had such high hopes earlier when she thought that shopping for love online might help her avoid her usual unsavoury choices.

As she scribbled furiously the tears returned and blotted out her words. She crumpled the paper, hurled another wasted dream to the ground and picked up another pristine sheet. She stared at it, unable to write.

She wrapped her arms around herself and massaged her hairline. A man entered, gliding through the chapel, his robes brushing the marble floor. He nodded his head toward the altar before progressing towards the prayer board. Under the watchful stony eyes of griffins, dragons and angels Jodie shrank yet deeper into the shadows.

The man's head turned from left to right as he

scrutinised the prayer board. Jodie's heart raced hoping he would move on but he lingered, still reading. A group of tourists entered and the man stopped reading and turned to them. Jodie willed him to move away but he turned back to the board and bent down. He picked up her discarded prayer from the floor. He placed it carefully on the table and very gently opened it, caressing its wrinkles back to its original form. He lifted the notice, read her words and nodded his head. She hoped the ground would swallow her. When it didn't, she opened her clenched fists and swollen eyes and raised her face. A knowing, baffled look met her gaze. A chord stirred within her and the anger and hopelessness that had unexpectedly brought her to this place of solace dissolved and she smiled. Halleluiah!

∽∾〇〇∾∾

*Magdalen College chapel can be accessed by visiting Magdalen College, High Street, Oxford. Whilst the college itself was built on this site in 1467, work on the chapel began in 1474 but the marble floor and bronze lectern are all that survive in the chapel from the seventeenth century restoration.*

# Lost and Found

## *Vicky Mancuso Brehm*

Charlotte followed the others into the silent college chapel with its high ceilings and rich wood panelling. There was a smell of musty hymn books. It was smaller, less grand, more intimate than the numerous other chapels the group had already been taken to. It made Charlotte feel at home.

In the background the tour guide's voice was like the roar of distant traffic, explaining the college's literary connections.

'. . . and William Tyndale, who courageously translated the Bible into English back in the sixteenth century, was one of the College's most famous alumni. Now I would like to move on fairly promptly to our next college, Magdalen. We will spend longer there, given its association with C. S. Lewis. Follow me everyone.'

The group was leaving. As Charlotte headed towards the door she noticed an unusual stained glass panel against the back wall of the chapel. It was illuminated from behind and portrayed a ponderous man wearing Tudor dress. Although the panel was traditional in its style, it looked new. A black and white cat was curled up asleep on a chair next to it, cosy on a soft cushion.

Outside in the summer sun the others were already leaving the quad. 'Why is the guide always in such a rush?' sighed Charlotte. That was the problem with the tour; there was no time to stop and enjoy the sights. The tour that in the brochure had sounded so appealing, consisted, instead, of ten days on a cramped coach, and rushing from sight to sight. Charlotte's blisters growing more painful by the day.

Derek had insisted that she should go without him. Charlotte wished he had wanted to come. She had gone, instead with her friend, Connie.

When Charlotte caught up with the group, they were just leaving Hertford College through the disproportionately large wooden doors. They turned right opposite the Bodleian Library, then right again towards the Bridge of Sighs where they stopped briefly to take photos. Charlotte reached into her handbag to take out her camera. It wasn't there.

'Connie,' Charlotte sighed, 'I must have left my camera in the college chapel . . . I'll have to go back for it.'

'The guide won't be pleased – there is no way she is going to wait for you. Why don't you meet us there?' suggested Connie, who was used to her friend's scatty ways. 'Make sure you keep your mobile on in case you get lost.'

Charlotte retraced her steps feeling a sudden relief at breaking free. She walked slowly. The giant blue cupola of the Radcliffe Camera glimmered majestically in the distance.

Back at Hertford, the soft green carpet of lawn shimmered in the July sunshine, the creepers on the buildings were vibrant as emeralds against the honey-coloured stone. Charlotte walked self-consciously past a group of people near the chapel entrance. Inside the chapel, she had a quick hunt around and found her camera next to the mysterious panel. The blisters on her feet were so sore. She sat down on one of the long wooden benches, relieved by the cool quietness, her mind swirling in a mixture of thoughts and prayers.

The black and white cat, now awake, tiptoed towards her meowing. It purred as she stroked its head.

'Hello pussy,' she said. The cat jumped up on to her lap. The two sat quietly like old friends. A moment of quiet after ten days of madness. A moment of perfect bliss.

Eventually the cat jumped down and trotted towards the door. Charlotte did not know how long she had been sitting there, but acknowledged reluctantly that it must be time to join the others. She followed the cat past the glass panel and out of the chapel. As she stepped out into the quad, her stomach churned with panic as she realised she had no idea which college they were going to next. What had the guide said? Was it Merton, or was that where they had been that morning? She vaguely recalled a mention of C. S. Lewis.

The cat stood next to her, rubbing its head against her leg. She looked up to see two women making their way towards her.

'Hello Simpkins!' said one of the women, smartly dressed and in her late twenties. She bent down to stroke her feline friend.

A waiter carrying a tray with drinks was coming towards them.

'Would you like some sherry?' he asked Charlotte.

'Oh! No thanks. I . . .' she hesitated for a moment.

'Would you prefer Pimms and lemonade?' enquired the waiter.

Pimms and lemonade sounded perfect in this beautiful place. Perhaps it was a thirst for freedom after ten days of being hostage to The Tour. Probably, it was because Derek was not there. He would have said 'No thanks, I am not with this group.'

'Yes please,' Charlotte heard herself say. The waiter handed her a fluted champagne glass full of a sparkling drink the colour of diluted caramel. She took a sip, tasting summer, garden parties and fruit.

The two young women re-surfaced from their conversation with Simpkins and both accepted drinks too.

'Hi. I'm Louise and this is Anne. We studied History from '95 to '98,' explained Louise.

'I'm Charlotte. Where are you from?'

The two friends told Charlotte they had travelled

from London for the day, where Louise worked as a lawyer. Anne had a job in marketing. They chatted for a while. Young, professional women living in London; they seemed to Charlotte like an exotic species. They were so different from Charlotte's friends back home who were middle-aged, predictable and safe, concerned with their kids and their ageing parents.

A smartly-dressed older man came over to introduce himself.

'I'm the new Principal, Roger Cornby-White.' His public school voice boomed out like a foghorn. He shook Charlotte's hand, rattling the bones in her arm. He had the beaming smile of a natural host, oozing confidence.

'I'm Charlotte, Charlotte Johnson.'

'Ah, one of our American friends! What did you study?'

'English.' Charlotte replied, convincing herself that it was not a lie. She had indeed studied English. At Iowa State University.

'English, excellent! There are a group of English graduates talking to Dr. Foster over there. I will make sure I introduce them to you at lunch.'

'Oh no,' Charlotte interjected, alarmed, 'I am not staying for lunch.'

'Nonsense, you must join us since you have come all this way.'

'No but . . .'

'I insist.'

'But you see I didn't . . .'

'I will have a word with the catering manager, I am sure they can squeeze in one more place.' And with that he marched off.

Charlotte stood, mouth open. What should she do? She could – and of course should – just leave. Or she could sit quietly at a table and be served lunch. She looked at what she was wearing. Apart from her sensible shoes, she was not exactly under-dressed; maybe she could get away with it.

The moment of decision crept up faster than she was expecting. The foghorn voice of the Principal was announcing that lunch was being served in the dining hall. People started to file past her to the far side of the quad.

They were heading for an extraordinary building. It looked like a circular staircase with windows following the curve of the stairs. The parallel rows of glass circled upwards like the stripes on a candy cane. Charlotte had decided. She set off with the crowd.

She circled giddily up the worn grey steps and into the oak-panelled dining hall. Three rows of tables the length of the hall were set for lunch, each place setting having a dizzying array of cutlery and a sparkling collection of glasses of different sizes. At the opposite end of the room was a perpendicular high table on a raised platform.

Another moment of panic: where should she sit?

'Come and sit with us,' offered Anne and Louise, sensing her hesitation.

'Thank you.' Charlotte shuffled behind them, her cheeks flushing as the reality of her deceit began to sink in.

She sat with Anne on one side and John, who had studied PPE, whatever that might be, on the other.

'Where are you from?' asked John.

'Iowa.'

'Did you see the article about Tyndale in The Economist a few months ago?'

Charlotte was speechless for a moment. 'No, I don't keep up with Hollywood that much,' she replied at last. John stared at her. Oh no, what had she said? Tyndale, why was the name so familiar?

'Yes, I read it,' Anne volunteered. 'I thought it was interesting how they compared Tyndale to modern-day political dissidents. An interesting theory, though stretching the facts somewhat.'

'Absolutely,' said John, giving up on Charlotte. 'Tyndale was not interested in politics. He did not set out to get into trouble with the authorities, that was just a consequence of his work.'

'Yes, and it was good to see him being given credit for his contribution to the development of the English language.'

'And it must have taken some perseverance to carry on with the work when he was receiving no credit for it, in fact quite the opposite,' continued John.

A waiter placed an elegantly arranged plate of melon

and port before Charlotte. It was delicious. John and Anne discussed Tyndale, then drifted into some detailed discussion on human rights issues and the role of the International Criminal Court in The Hague.

Charlotte sat back and enjoyed the conversation, the atmosphere, the jokes and the waiter-service. She felt relaxed. Maybe it was the Pimms. Maybe it was just this deep yet ridiculous sense of feeling that she fitted in. Her life back home, the suburban house, the double garage, the housework, teaching Dickens to her disinterested pupils, seemed so bland. Of course she loved everyone back home. But this was exciting; eating a three-course meal in the middle of the day, talking of politics and literature, meeting these people from a different world. She wished she were twenty again.

The main course of roast duck was served. Charlotte had not eaten duck before; it tasted good.

'Ladies and Gentlemen,' broke forth the voice of the Principal standing up to give a speech as dessert was being served.

'Let me welcome you back to the College, on this auspicious occasion, the dedication of the Tyndale panel in the College Chapel. We are honouring one of the College's most famous alumni today for his courage and conviction, which he paid for with his life.'

The Principal paused, his strong face suddenly serious.

'We are pleased to commemorate his bravery with the new stained-glass panel in the Chapel. Thank you each and every one for your generous contributions.' The audience applauded. The Principal went on to explain the process of commissioning and installing the panel, before proposing a toast.

'To William Tyndale and the Hertford Alumni Association.' Everyone in the hall rose and raised their glasses in a toast.

When lunch was over, people started to drift reluctantly out of the hall, condensing years of their lives into tiny fragments of conversation. Charlotte followed the crowd down the circular staircase and out into the bright sunshine and gaudy green of the quad.

The Principal approached her.

'Have you seen the Tyndale panel yet?'

'Why, I don't think so,' Charlotte replied, unsure. Uncertainty was the wrong approach to take with the Principal.

'Let me show you before you go.' He led her into the chapel and pointed to the glass panel that Charlotte had seen earlier.

'I think it is very fitting.' The Principal sounded like a proud father. Simpkins was back on his chair next to the panel, fast asleep.

After a few minutes admiring the panel, the Principal turned to say goodbye.

'Lovely to see you. You must come to another reunion next time you are over,' said the Principal, shaking her hand.

Standing next to the portrait of a man of such

integrity was making Charlotte feel uncomfortable. Her conscience was running on overtime under Tyndale's steady gaze.

'I'm afraid there has been a misunderstanding.' The words seemed to be making their own way out of her mouth.

'Oh?'

'You see, I didn't study English here at all. I studied at Iowa State University. I tried to explain . . . I am so sorry about lunch, I will settle up with the College . . .'

'Oh! You mean I dragged you up to lunch . . .' The Principal stared at her motionless. 'No, it is I who must apologise,' he said. 'My wife says I never listen to anyone. Yes, I recall now, you did try to tell me you weren't staying for lunch. So what brought you to Hertford?'

Charlotte felt her cheeks warming. 'I have come on a literary tour of Oxford.'

'A tour? You mean you are a tourist?'

Principal Cornby-White roared with laughter. 'You must come again! Why you are practically an honorary member now!'

Charlotte looked up at the portrait. It seemed that even Tyndale had a smile on his face.

໖ຉໂ

*Nestling opposite the Bodleian Library on Catte Street, little Hertford College traces its origins to Elias de Hertford's Hart Hall, founded in the late thirteenth century. It was upgraded to Hertford College in 1874, thanks to its benefactor the financier*

*Sir Thomas Baring. In the following fifty years, the College was rebuilt and gained some architectural gems, such as its Hall with its unusual spiral staircase and the iconic bridge over the New College Lane that joins two of the College's quads.*

*William Tyndale studied at the then Hart Hall in the sixteenth century at the height of the Reformation. Tyndale spent his life translating the Bible into English, but did not live to see his work completed. Condemned as a heretic, after years spent in hiding he was eventually martyred in Brussels in 1536. Nevertheless Tyndale's translation formed the basis of the first New Testament in English and later the complete Bible in English, printed very shortly after his death.*

*The commemorative stained glass panel depicting Tyndale is on display in Hertford College's chapel. The spiral staircase and dining hall where Charlotte had lunch are on the left as you come into Hertford's main quad. Both can be accessed through the College's main entrance on Catte Street.*

# Buckland and the Antediluvian Hyena's Den

## S. A. Edwards

### Oxford 1823

The Reverend William Buckland was not a vain man; in fact, in some quarters he was considered careless of his appearance. His only vanity was his magnificent eyebrows. They were brilliant white, and framed his brow with an extravagant curl extending two inches from his forehead. The furthest tips of them were tinted a pale yellow from the nicotine from his pipe. Buckland used his eyebrows as a means of communication, similar to a rock hopper penguin. Waggled they expressed pleasure. Lowered they expressed displeasure.

He was sitting in his study sipping a cup of tea and nibbling at toast while Mrs Buckland stood companionably behind him combing the eyebrow dandruff from them. As she combed, snowflakes of dandruff drifted and settled onto the ginger fur of the large cat sleeping on Buckland's knee. The cat would be devastated when it noticed, and it would take over an hour's thorough washing to restore its coat to its customary high standard.

Recently Buckland had been studying his pigeons, and had come to the conclusion that mutual grooming strengthens the pair bond. Mrs Buckland held the view that there was not much mutual about this eyebrow grooming activity but for reasons of marital harmony kept her views to herself. Her silence Buckland took to mean 'pair bond reinforced', and he was happily writing in his head a treatise entitled 'Observations of the effects of mutual grooming and the calming effect on the wives of clergymen', when their moment of marital harmony was broken by a knock at the door. The maid stuck her head in and said in a resigned voice,

'There's a man at the door with a hyena.'

'Splendid,' shouted Buckland leaping from his chair.

### December 1822

Yorkshire is a long way away.

Buckland was on his way to Kirkland Cave in Yorkshire. He had received a letter from a Mr Billy Braithwaite informing him that the said gentleman had found some bones in a cave that might be of interest to him. Big bones, odd bones, and that he, Mr Braithwaite, had heard that Mr Buckland was a collector of natural history, and that for the small remuneration of five guineas he would take Buckland to them. Buckland replied by return that he was on his way.

In Buckland's absence, Christ Church and Oxford breathed a sigh of relief and settled down to enjoy the peace and quiet.

The journey was to take two weeks, not the two days advised by the Royal Turnpike Association handbook and gazetteer in its route-finder section. This was mainly because Buckland could not pass an open rock face without leaping down to examine every fallen pebble. Bess, his black mare, had grown so accustomed to this behaviour that she stopped of her own volition whether Buckland wanted her to or not. This trait made her a hopeless mount to anyone other than Buckland. As they approached Kirkland, Bess's plod had slowed more than usual, due to the extra stones she was carrying in her saddle bags.

Billy Braithwaite, accompanied by his dog, led Buckland over the slippery clints and grikes towards the entrance to the cave eighty feet up the cliff face. The mouth of the cave was hidden by a thicket of wind-pruned blackthorn. They carried sacks, hammers, a lantern and two rounds of ham sandwiches prepared by Mrs Braithwaite.

'Well, are you ready?' Braithwaite enquired.

Buckland tucked his trousers into his socks and said, 'Ready.'

Thus prepared, the explorers entered the mouth of the cave. It was pitch dark, lit only by the trembling light from Braithwaite's lantern. His dog followed, its natural exuberance curbed by the gloom of the place. The roof of the cave lowered, and as they progressed, they were forced to crawl on their hands and knees. They squeezed through a fissure in the limestone to emerge in a cavern.

It was silent, other than the rhythmic drip of water from a stalactite on to the stalagmites below. Mud sucked at their boots as they walked.

Billy Braithwaite placed the lantern on the ground. The candle light flickered in the draught but illuminated the floor of the cave. They were standing on hundreds of bones, bones of all shapes and sizes. Skulls, clavicles, scapulas, tarsals, metatarsals, hooves, femurs, horns, fragments, shards, splinters, and thousands of teeth. To Buckland's joy, he thought he could see the remnants of a tusk. His mind raced. What was he looking at?

The first bone Buckland picked up was the jaw bone of an ass. Next he found the shoulder blade of a mastodon, then a deer antler, the foot of a tapir and then – joy of joys – small round pebble-like nuggets, with small bones and splinters visible within them.

'Look, look, perfectly preserved album graecum,' he called excitedly to Billy Braithwaite.

'Looks like a turd to me,' replied Braithwaite.

'That is the layman's term for them, I believe.'

Braithwaite's dog was having a good time as well. It had never seen so many bones. It picked one up and gave it an exploratory gnaw, but gave up after a few minutes, disappointed at the absence of marrow.

'Hyena's skull, definitely. A hyena skull,' said Buckland handing the specimen to Braithwaite to put in his sack. He picked up the bone the dog had been chewing. 'Look at the teeth marks on this. They look so fresh. Gnu leg bone, obviously a gnu, an idiot could tell this was a gnu. Look at the gnu-ness of it. It's been worried by something with incredibly powerful jaws. Teeth marks made by a pack of hyenas, do you think?'

Braithwaite shrugged, and kicked the dog out of the way.

They worked collecting bones for three hours. When the sack was so heavy Braithwaite could barely lift it, they stopped.

It was raining as they emerged from the cave, penetrating Yorkshire rain.

'On the same day all the fountains of the great deep were broken up, and the windows of heaven were opened, and the rain was upon the earth forty days and forty nights,' quoted Buckland, as they trudged back down the moor.

'Aye, thae's in Yorkshire now, lad,' responded Braithwaite.

For a moment the sun broke through the clouds, illuminating the drizzle. Buckland gasped. 'It's a sign,' he shouted to the retreating backs of Braithwaite and the dog.

'Daft sod,' thought Braithwaite.

## August 1823

In his study in Corpus Christi, Buckland sat and thought. The specimens he had collected revealed themselves, after much study, to be bones of hippopotami, elephant, rhinoceros, bison, tiger, gnu, elk, wolf, rat, bird, mouse and hyena, lots of hyenas. These bones were now pinned for reference on the walls of his study, giving it the look of a Zoroastrian ossuary, a look Buckland had always admired.

His large brain ran round and round the problem, worrying at it, herding it into shape, only for it to make a run for it and the solution to scatter. He wrote:

'Hypothesis'. Then wrote: 'Hyena's skull, hyena's teeth, gnu bones (and assorted others, some animals extinct, none native to England) with teeth marks. Were the animals eaten by hyenas? These animals are not native to the British Isles, so how had they got there? How old are they?'

What was the answer to all these mysterious questions?

He imagined three thousand years ago the fetid darkness of the cave. A pack of savage hyenas fighting over the carcass of the elephant they had dragged back to their lair, the snarling the gnashing of teeth. A scene similar to the dining room in Christ Church on roast dinner night.

He doodled for a bit. Drank some tepid tea, chewed a crust of toast left over from elevenses, and stroked the cat. Then he looked out of the window. In Christ Church meadow he could see Wombwell and Bostocks Beast Show setting up camp.

The Beast Show arrived every year in time for the St Giles's Fair. The brightly coloured caravans of the artistes piped smoke from their chimneys, as they fried bacon for their dinners. The sound of lions roaring, camels braying, and elephants trumpeting, echoed across the lawns of

Christ Church.

Gladys Bickerstaff, stage name Queen Nefertiti, the jewel of the Orient, snake charmer, was feeding live rats to her boa constrictors. The day after they had been fed, they were uncomfortable to work with, as the body of the rat pressed awkwardly against her liver when the snake wrapped itself around her middle. So she liked to get it over and done with a few days before the show opened.

The smell of the animals drifted into Buckland's study and the cat looked subdued. Mrs Buckland came in with some fresh tea.

'Do you think hyenas could drag an elephant into a cave?' she asked helpfully. He ignored her.

She pressed on. 'Do hyenas eat hippopotamuses?'

He pretended he hadn't heard. How was a man to concentrate with a woman babbling on like that? He did some more thinking. Fed the tortoise, smoked a pipe, calmed his mind by re-arranging his fly collection and then he GOT IT.

What he needed was a live hyena. He could then compare the marks made by the teeth of the living hyena with the teeth marks on the bones from the cave. If they matched, and he was confident they would, he would have found, as he suspected, an antediluvian hyena's den.

But he didn't have a hyena. His eye was drawn again out of the window to the distant bustle of the Beast Show.

Mr. Bostock could barely believe his luck when he read the note from Buckland. Yes, he did have a hyena.

And it was ancient, decrepit, it smelt, it had rotten teeth, it was moth-eaten, incontinent. It cringed when anyone approached. It was a surprisingly fussy eater, and in protest at the quality of food Mr Bostock fed it, had eaten its own front leg, so now it hopped. It was now so repellent that no-one was prepared to pay the sixpence he charged to look at it, and the thing was a bloody nuisance. He'd be glad to see the back of it. He had a plan to replace the hyena with a more commercial coypu, and advertise it as 'The biggest rat in the world'. Now who wouldn't pay to see that?

He arrived at the door of Buckland's study with the three-legged animal at his side. It urinated on the mat.

When Buckland first saw the hyena, it was love at first sight.

'I'll take it,' he told Mr Bostock, grasping the piece of string that served as its lead. 'A spotted cape hyena. Is it a male or a female?' he asked.

Bostock blushed, 'It's hard to tell, sir.'

Buckland waggled his eyebrows in astonishment. 'You mean you don't know. Didn't your mother teach you about the birds and the bees?'

'I mean, you can't tell, sir. You can't tell girl hyenas from boy hyenas, because they both have . . .', and here Mr Bostock looked exceedingly embarrassed, having to use this word in front of a man of the cloth, '. . . pinkles'.

'Pinkles?' asked Buckland, baffled.

'Podgers,' Bostock tried again.

'Sorry, I'm not with you?'

Bostock, shifting from foot to foot, mumbled, 'Pizzles.'

Buckland looked ecstatic. 'Are you telling me that if she is female, she has a pseudo-penis?'

Bostock scratched his head and said 'I think so.'

So Hermaphrodite, which is what Buckland called her, came to live in the kennels of Corpus Christi College. Buckland fed her on the finest cow bones the college's butcher, Mr Grimshaw, could supply. Buckland took her for walks around Oxford. She became something of a celebrity.

Buckland made a forensic study of the teeth marks found on Hermaphrodite's leftovers. He compared these with the marks found on the bones from the cave. He concluded that the origin of the marks on both sets of bones were indeed from hyenas, as he had first thought. He compared Hermaphrodite's fresh faeces with the album graeca from the cave, and concluded they too were from the same source. And how had this den of hyenas with all its extinct animals come to be in England? Buckland decided that the only plausible explanation given the evidence was that the cave, the hyenas and the remains of their prey, all animals of darkest Africa, not native to England, had been drowned in the deluge sent by God to destroy the earth (Book of Genesis, Chapter 6):

'When Noah was six hundred years old, God, saddened at the wickedness of mankind, decided to send a great deluge to destroy all life. And so the Flood came, and all life was extinguished, except for those who were with Noah.'

Buckland felt all goose bumpy. He had hanging on his study walls the actual remains of the animals who didn't walk in two by two. This was going to be one of the most exciting scientific discoveries of the century. It would nip in the bud the ridiculous theory of Rev. Henslow of Cambridge and his latest protégé a youth called Darwin, that we were all descended from monkeys.

Unknown to Buckland, poor rotten-toothed Hermaphrodite could only suck the juices out of the bones she was given. When no one was watching, the pack of Foxhounds in the next door kennel organised bone raids, rioting into Hermaphrodite's cage to have a gnaw at her supper, before being beaten back into their own quarters by the whippers-in.

*Also published in Tell Tails edited by Wendy Greenberg*

ॐ✸✸ॐ

*Buckland's best-selling book,* Reliquiae Diluviana; or Observations on the Organic Remains Contained in Caves, Fissures and Diluvial Gravel, and on Other Geological Phenomena Attesting the Action of a Universal Deluge, *published in 1823, establishes in Buckland's own words 'the universality of a recent inundation of the earth, as no difficulties or objections that have hitherto arisen are in any way sufficient to overrule'. Some of this story is true and the bits that aren't should be. Visit Buckland's hyena's skull in the Oxford Museum of Natural History. See Hermaphrodite the stuffed hyena in the Oxford Museum of Natural History. Visit Corpus Christi. Read Reliquiae Diluviana on line at www.googlebooks*

# Women Drivers

## *Wendy Greenberg*

A bigail had long been dreaming of her new mini. It had to be a shopping trip for its maiden voyage.

After several tours round Oxford's ring road, they reached the city centre. Abigail tucked into a tight spot in the Westgate car park.

Shopped-out, they returned in the early evening. Abigail inspected her new baby adoringly and they piled in through the passenger door. She was parked up against a concrete pillar and her anxious manoeuvrings brought them closer still.

'All out' – the girls took a corner each. 'Bend and lift'.

Once re-positioned, it was easy to drive off, laughing!

❧⊰∙ℬ⊙ℭℬ∙⊱❧

*Oxford is famous for producing the Mini at the Cowley car works. The Westgate car park is a rather less proud creation but somewhere you can leave your car and enjoy central Oxford. Park better than Abigail!*

# From Magdalen Bridge

## *Andrew Bax*

'Mother!' Helen was outraged. 'If you are trying to tell me what I think you are trying to tell me – I don't want to know!' She reached for the pole and angrily pushed the punt away from the bank.

But she did want to know – very much indeed. Not this particular detail perhaps, but anything else about her father would be welcome. Like where he was now and why he had never been in touch. And if he really went to America, destined to become rich and famous as her mother claimed, why was there no trace of him? Googling 'Danny McLeod', in all its variations in spelling, brought up over 14,000 entries but none of them graduated from Magdalen College in 1987. Whenever his name was mentioned Ruth would say 'We were just a bit careless', to which Helen retorted, 'Thanks Mother – that makes me feel really wanted', and a frosty silence would descend on them. It descended now.

As Helen grappled inexpertly with the pole, Ruth,

lost in dewy-eyed reminiscence, glanced back at the little cutting they had just left. That was the spot all right. All those years ago, the willows had seemed to fold around them like curtains. Just her, Danny and the punt. It was a beautiful evening in June, starting to get dark but still warm. And so was the champagne they had brought with them. She sighed: they were just a bit careless.

But, she reminded herself, things had turned out all right in the end. Pregnancy and the responsibility of parenthood somehow ignited ambition in her and, instead of settling for the quiet teaching job she was expecting, she embarked on a career in research, eventually joining the University of Auckland. Now she was back in Oxford with Helen, her 22-year old daughter, to lecture on 'The Impact of the Digital Age on Remote Polynesian Communities'. She could hardly believe it.

At last night's conference party, an earnest young man had asked about the opportunities in New Zealand when Helen's lively laugh rang out from across the room. At once, Ruth was reminded of Danny. It sounded so like him and, like him, Helen was the life and soul of every party.

Helen had been trying to fend off the attentions of a crusty old don who seemed to have been at Magdalen for ever, so she asked, 'Do you happen to remember an undergraduate called Danny McLeod? He was here about twenty years ago.'

'McLeod? Never forget him. Kept arguing in my tutorials – damn nuisance. Always in trouble – usually high on alcohol or other substances. Quite brilliant, though.'

'What happened to him?'

'Went to America, I think. Probably made billions on Wall Street. Or maybe he's a top prof at Harvard. He was going to make his mark, whatever he did.' So what her mother had told her was true. But why was he so untraceable?

That morning, while her mother was at the conference, Helen called in at the bursar's office. 'McLeod? 1987? Yes – here he is.' The assistant sifted through some files. 'That's funny. We have nothing on him after graduation. We keep a record of all our graduates. Appointments and distinctions – public domain stuff like that, but we can't pass on contact details – Data Protection Act, you know.' She carried on sifting. 'It's extraordinary. Even our dullest drop-out does something in later life which is recorded in our files.' She paused. 'But, by all accounts, he certainly had a busy life when he was here. Although he was marked down as a trouble-maker – protests, demonstrations – that sort of thing, he seems to have been very gifted academically, when he put his mind to it.' Then she laughed. 'During his last week, the President's bicycle was found hanging from the flag pole. No evidence of course, but the finger of suspicion pointed at your Mr McLeod' she added with a smile.

In the meantime, Ruth had slipped out of the conference to make her own enquiries. She knew that if you wanted to know anything in Oxford, you didn't ask the authorities, you asked the college porters. The man at the lodge called over his shoulder, ' 'ere Bill! You were here in '87. Remember a bloke called Danny McLeod?'

Bill looked up from the *Sun*, and a grin spread slowly across his face. 'Remember him? I'll say I remember him. He kept giving me racing tips. None of them any good – not one. How can I help you madam?'

'Do you know what he did when he left Oxford? I thought he went to America.'

'Yes, he did. But he came back. Things didn't work out for him over there. Anyway, he was having too much fun in Oxford, I reckon.'

Ruth groped for something to hold on to. 'And where is he now?' she stammered.

'Don't know. See him around sometimes. Things don't seem to have worked out much better here. Are you all right madam?'

Conflicting emotions threatened to overwhelm her but she pulled herself together and went back to the conference. Distracted now by the possibility that Danny could be in Oxford, she contributed little to the debate on neo-materialism. What would she do if she met him? He probably wouldn't recognise her – probably he'd forgotten all about her. What would she say? 'Hello Danny, may I introduce you to your daughter?' She tried to look forward to the evening's punting with Helen.

Now, as Helen struggled with the punt pole, Ruth told her about Parson's Pleasure where a high fence and its notice, 'Ladies to Alight Here', had protected the modesty of men who chose to bathe naked.

All those years ago, Danny had persuaded Ruth to

stay in the punt while he poled it through the gap and she lay giggling in the bottom. Now there was no sign of the fence or any indication of its past secrets, but their special place, just below it, was still there.

A sudden lurch made Ruth turn to see Helen grimly holding on to the pole which had stuck in the mud. 'Let go – you'll fall in' she called, as the punt nudged backwards into the bank. She was glad to see that the frost had melted and that Helen was laughing. Danny had had the same slight build, high cheeks and aquiline nose; the same wicked grin and sparkling eyes, even the same shoulder-length hair.

'There's a man selling ice creams at the boathouse. If we get back let's have one.'

'What do you mean – if? I was just getting the hang of it.'

The pole was still stuck fast in the mud as they drifted away. It was retrieved by a noisy punt-load of tourists.

Helen, back in control, had the punt pointing in the right direction and Magdalen Tower was occasionally visible through the trees.

The last time Ruth had seen Danny he had been bursting with excitement as he pointed to the flagpole from which a bicycle was suspended – 'I did it for you,' he said. Then it was the end of term; he was going to America and promised to stay in touch, but he didn't. She never had any serious relationships after that. Who wants to be saddled with another man's daughter?

More expertly now, Helen steered the punt into a vacant slot at the Magdalen Bridge Boathouse and looked up at the parapet high above her.

'You didn't jump from that, did you? You must have been crazy!'

'I did and I was,' Ruth smiled.

It was here that she first met Danny. May Morning 1987: cold and drizzly but thronged with people who had been partying all night. On the spur of the moment, she had climbed over the wall and, with her silk dress billowing over her head, had jumped. The shock of cold water sobered her instantly and a laughing undergraduate, even more sodden that she was, waded over to help her out. It was Danny.

Helen joined the ice cream queue. 'Chocolate mint chip and a raspberry ripple, please,' she said, as she rummaged through the unfamiliar currency in her purse.

'I'm sorry – I've sold out of those but . . .,' the man was saying.

Helen looked up at him. There was something familiar about his thin features, but she didn't like his long, lank hair. Funny little man – and why was he staring over her shoulder like that? He looked as if he'd seen a ghost. She turned to see her mother staring back, the blood draining from her face.

'Helen,' Ruth gasped 'I don't think I want one after all. I'm suddenly feeling a bit . . . faint.' She began to walk quickly away. 'Sorry dear. I need to lie down.' Helen shrugged apologetically to the ice cream man and followed her mother.

Shaking now, the ice cream man called for his

colleague to take over and rushed out of the kiosk. Minutes later he sank against an ancient willow on the river bank, and gulped from the bottle he always had with him.

When the street lights came on he was still sitting there, still shaking. And the bottle was empty.

༺ঌৎঌ঺

*Ruth and Danny's moment of carelessness took place where a drainage channel joins the Cherwell, just below Parson's Pleasure. This venerable institution, about which John Betjeman remarked '. . . There may be many parsons there, for all we can tell – clergymen are a great feature of North Oxford – but everyone is naked. Bodies lie stretched on the grass, looking up between the poplars, pipes jammed into mouths, sunlight dappling bald or long-haired heads.' It was a notorious amenity when Ruth and Danny were undergraduates but the dead hand of regulation forced it to close in 1991. Nevertheless it remains part of Oxford's folklore, spawning many anecdotes, such as the occasion when a group of young ladies punted through, causing much consternation among the men; all covered their modesty except one, who covered his head, explaining that 'In Oxford, I am recognised by my face.' Magdalen College and Magdalen Bridge are among Oxford's most iconic buildings, and are the scene for world-famous May Morning celebrations. On 1 May for nearly 500 years, the Magdalen College Choir has greeted the dawn with a hymn sung from the top of the tower. These days it is almost inaudible to the revellers below, many of whom have been partying all night and are far from sober. A more recent tradition has been to jump from the bridge into the Cherwell, as Ruth and Danny did, a practice which has now become quite dangerous because the river is so shallow. People have been hiring punts from Magdalen Bridge Boathouse for nearly a century. It is reached from a slipway next to the college itself and it is from the kiosk there that Helen went to buy ice creams.*

# Tree Study, Boars Hill

## Kathleen Daly

Ellie made her way past the precarious brick wall, over the tree-lined muddy bottom, and up the sandy track. The pale mist of a bonfire drifted across the path, stinging her nostrils. Today she was going to draw the tree. She had wanted this since she had first brought her children, whimpering with fatigue, or fast asleep in the back pack, along this bridleway. Now that they were teenagers and could walk on their own, they still had no inclination to come with her, but she could finally carry out her plan.

Why had she put it off so long? As a child, Ellie had loved drawing. It was her way of capturing reality, of making sense of the world, or at least escaping from it. When there had been rows, when her father had shouted and her mother had stormed out of the house, she had crept up to her bedroom and taken out her pad and pencils. When her parents had separated, there had been no money to send her to art college. She had been realistic, and taken an office job. She had given away her paints and pencils, afraid her desire to draw would overcome her common sense. After her marriage to Keith, money was not a problem, but the children arrived and she still had no time.

Keith. She still felt the numb vacancy of his absence. For months she had been stupefied. Only the children had kept her going. This summer she had started to emerge from her chrysalis, to take a new interest in life. Not that the grief had gone away, it had just receded, gradually, out of the forefront of her consciousness.

This autumn was a resurrection. She could distinguish colours and shapes instead of a dull grey mass. Underfoot the rusty carpet of last year's leaves was degrading into humus. New arrivals stippled it crimson, russet, gilt. The underside of a fallen leaf glowed white in a shaft of sunlight. She drank in the textures of the trees: the ghostly pallor of birch bark, the warty excrescences of chestnut, the limb-smooth skin of sycamore splashed with bright orange lichen, the parasitic arteries of ivy.

But this tree was special. It seemed immemorial, a relic of some uprooted, ancient hedge, left to fend for itself in an empty field. It had the pewter patina of driftwood stranded on a green shore. Time had eroded it to the shape of a dancer, its branches twisted in frozen motion, pointing to the sky. The trunk was hollow. The children had once hidden there in games of tag, shrieking with delight when discovered. They had clambered over its branches, poked their fingers into its crevices. Beyond its stark silhouette clustered the barns and farmhouse of Chilswell, set against the distant tower of Magdalen College and the dome of the Radcliffe Camera .

Today the light was ideal. It had that transparent quality peculiar to spring and autumn, that dissolves shadows and makes the world a two-dimensional stage-set. She wanted to capture that perfect moment when the sun had burnt away the mist, before the afternoon clouds dulled the light's intensity.

She emerged from the tunnel of trees, went through the metal horse-gate. She stared at the neighbouring wood, at the farm, into the distance, anywhere but at the tree. She wanted to creep up on her prey, prowl round it, surprise it. She wanted to savour the moment when she found the best view, the view that gave her volume and depth, the play of light and shadow on and around her tree. She noted how the landscape had changed since she was here last. The farm itself had gone, its buildings converted into fine houses with red or grey roofs, set in wide grounds. The slurry pond was now a clear lake with dabchicks and moorhens. The field was empty of cows.

She turned to look at her tree. At first she was puzzled. Something had changed, but what? The hawthorn hedge was still there at the side. A charm of goldfinches quested through teasel stems. A jay flashed its white rump. She heard the harsh yaffle of a green woodpecker. The picture frame was empty. Instead of her subject, there was only negative space, grass below, and above, pale blue sky.

For a moment Ellie stood frozen. Then she felt a harsh, hot prickling in her eyes. I mustn't cry, I mustn't, she insisted silently, it's only a tree, don't be stupid, don't be stupid. But somehow all that accumulated grief, Keith's death, the children growing up, those wasted years without pencil and paint, surged up and burst its banks. She wanted to howl, howl. She slumped on a pile of wood, head cradled in her hands, shutting out the light. She lost track of time. It was the chill that brought her to her senses. The sun had gone in now.

She had come so far, she told herself. She had all her pencils, her sketchpad. She had nothing else. There must be something she could draw. Perhaps another tree? She had seen so many on her way. She had thought, I will capture you, but another time, after I have my tree. She didn't have the energy to go back now, to settle for second-best. She looked around her. She was marooned on the shipwreck of her tree. She recognised the twist of the topmost limb, the curve of the downward branch. She picked up her pencil and, without taking her eye from the bark or looking at the paper, she began to draw.

٭☙⊙☙٭

*The tree that inspired this story is still standing opposite Chilswell Farm. To follow in Ellie's footsteps, take a bus to Boars Hill, or by car or bicycle, leave Oxford by the Abingdon Road, take the Southern Bypass and at the roundabout, the second exit to Wootton (Hinksey Hill). At the Y-junction, take the right turn into Foxcombe Lane (not the Abingdon turn). The view opens up through fields on your right, towards the 'Dreaming Spires'. Just after these fields, turn right into Berkeley Road, past the Open University offices in Foxcombe Hall on your left. Buses from Oxford stop here. Continue along this road (Jarn Way). Jarn Mound will be on your right. Pass the bridleway next to it (which is often muddy), and take the next bridleway along the little road to the right, past a field with a friendly horse. This is known as 'Matthew Arnold's Field'. You will come out in The Ridgeway (watch out for traffic). Almost opposite is a very narrow bridleway (which can be muddy), with a tall brick wall on the right hand side. This leads you down through a wood, along a tree-fringed path beside some fields on the left, and to the horse-gate. Go through this gate and you will see the tree at the bottom of the hill. But hurry! Since the author first saw it a decade ago, the tree has gradually shed its bark and branches, and looks fragile enough for the next autumn gale to topple it altogether.*

# *Whatever it Takes*

## *Jackie Vickers*

Harriet's aunt has written from Holloway Goal. Aunt Louisa has brought dishonour to her family by chaining herself to some railings. Harriet, however, admires her courage and has been hoping for some words of advice. Louisa has written at length of the 'Cause', fighting for justice and women's rights, and only at the end of her letter does she exhort her niece to 'do whatever it takes'.

Harriet is disappointed, she had hoped for something more specific. Her aunt, after all, is a woman of action, whose suffragette friends make plans and are decisive. She wants to be told what to do, as she feels her own life has become intolerable. Three years have passed since an eminent artist came to dine and remarked on her exceptional talent as he flipped through her sketchbook. Harriet has pleaded, raged and sulked, but her parents are unyielding, even though the Ruskin School of Drawing and Fine Art is only a short walk away. She takes up Louisa's letter again and reads it more carefully. This time she decides the phrase 'do whatever it takes' can be understood as a battle cry.

Harriet is familiar with the Ashmolean Galleries. She spends most mornings there drawing some exhibit, or making a careful study of a painting. Her mother believes she is examining the latest fashions on display, or exchanging secrets with a friend as they walk in the University Parks. Before she leaves today, Harriet stands for a while by the stairs to the upper galleries and watches the students come and go. Then she walks over to their notice board. She has an idea.

A few days later, Harriet is standing in the deep shadow cast by the museum portico. She has rolled up her fashionably long, navy jacket and removed her hat. She pulls a tight bundle from her capacious bag and shakes out the shabby coat and hat she has taken from their servant's room. She repeats her aunt's words to herself, 'whatever it takes, whatever it takes'. A student leads her to a room where a tall, bearded man is bent over some drawings on a large table. The man waves her towards a folding screen which stands by a large sofa, covered with a white sheet.

'Take your clothes off,' he says, barely looking at her.

Harriet places her sketch-book on the table in front of him and goes to undress. She is shaking and has difficulty undoing all her buttons and hooks. Looking through a crack in the screen she sees that the man has picked up her sketch-book and is examining the drawings, taking them to the tall windows for a closer look. Harriet has now removed all her clothes and is taking deep breaths to control her shivering. She pulls the pins from her hair, which tumbles over her back and shoulders, a thick mass of golden curls. Then she moves to the sofa and sits down, covering herself with her arms.

He turns and frowns a little.

'You're a little on the thin side,' he remarks, and leans forward to lift her arm along the curved back. Then he tells her to lie down, and adjusts her legs.

'You'll have to stop trembling and loosen up a bit if you come to work here.' His voice is stern, but Harriet notices a faint smile about his mouth, as he gently runs his fingers along her thigh.

After she has dressed he waves the sketch-book at her.

'Where did you find this?' he shows her the cover with her name, Harriet Winter, 35 Bardwell Road, across the top in bold black letters. 'I am going there to dinner tonight,' he adds, looking confused.

'I know,' she replies. 'I am Harriet Winter.'

A look of horror passes across his face. She watches him as he drops into an armchair and rests his head in his hands. When he finally looks up, she sees the parts of his face not covered by beard are now a greenish-white and beaded with sweat.

'Did anyone see you come in here?'

'Quite a few,' Harriet says. 'A red-haired student showed me to your room; I should know him anywhere.'

Professor Rothermere struggles out of his chair and paces up and down, looking at the floor. His collapse has given Harriet the confidence to say, 'You haven't asked me why I am here.'

'To put me in a compromising position, I suppose.'

Harriet ignores this and says in the gentle, educated tones of north Oxford, 'I should be very grateful if you would take me on as a student, here at the Ruskin.'

The professor looks at her, surprised. 'But there would be no difficulty, your drawings indicate remarkable talent,' and he starts flicking through her drawings to stop the tremor in his hands.

'My parents refuse to allow it,' Harriet says in a hard voice. He frowns, not understanding.

'This can easily be resolved without anyone knowing.' Harriet nods towards the sofa. 'Tonight I shall have a migraine, so be reassured, I shall not be present at dinner. May I look forward to receiving an offer of a place at the Ruskin?'

'But if your parents disapprove,' he says helplessly.

Harriet looks him in the eye.

'It is now in your hands, Professor Rothermere. You must do whatever it takes.'

Harriet Winter's paintings are much sought-after these days and are mostly held in private collections. She lives in a small house in Jericho, which has an attic studio lit by skylights. On one wall hangs a Rothermere, a gift from the artist. It is called Reclining Nude reading a letter.

৵৵ঙ৻ঔ৵৶

*The Ruskin School of Drawing and Fine Art was founded in 1871 by John Ruskin and stayed in the Ashmolean Galleries until 1974 when it moved to its current premises at 74 High Street. The museum galleries have recently been remodelled and display, among other things, a fine collection of paintings. Unfortunately the Ashmolean has not yet purchased any works by Rothermere or Winter.*

# The Bottle's Refrain

## Nichola May

It is Friday. Noon. 37 degrees the radio says. In the cavern below the hotel it is a semitone cooler. Pierre scans his next customer. Will it be an aromatic Riesling? A floral Chianti? The walls vibrate with a hundred bottles. A good waiter – and Pierre is one of the best – can select a single voice from the chorus.

Delighted with his choice he galliards across the floor: 'Today for you, Madame, Monsieur, I recommend this.'

It is Friday. 2pm. 36 degrees. They say it may rain later. Pierre serves the afternoon customers cappuccino, espresso, Americano, tea. Mostly tea. The English never drink wine in the afternoon unless they are celebrating. In this city it is only students who celebrate.

It is Friday. 3.30pm. 34 degrees. The lunchtime crowd have moved on, some to their hotel rooms, others to sightsee and complain about the heat. In the brasserie a man dozes behind his newspaper. A woman wheels her suitcase through towards reception and startles him.

It is Friday. 6.30pm. 25 degrees. The radio says it has been the hottest day this year. Pierre watches the gyrations of flying ants as they reel up from the courtyard. The tables fill. Pierre offers Beaujolais, the customer wants Sancerre. Some want lemonade. Some prefer beer. They want ice like this, lemon like that – in that glass, not this one. Pierre thinks it is the heat.

It is Friday. 9.30pm. 22 degrees. The breeze outside whips up a discarded tourist leaflet and spins it around the courtyard. Pierre wipes the bar, stacks menus. Today in the brasserie a business deal has been conceded, a lover proposed to, a home left, but all that remains as evidence are fingerprints on empty bottles.

It is Friday. 11.45pm. 20 degrees. Rain is falling in the courtyard. Pierre cleans two glasses and places them symmetrically on a corner table. He moves two chairs into perfect alignment. From the rack at the back of the bar he listens, selects one bottle and removes the cork. He lights a candle, removes his apron and waits.

It is Saturday. 1.14 am. 18 degrees. She is here. Her hair strays from the band she has tied it back with. Her umbrella is folded and dripping. She carries a small case, a new one he hasn't seen before. He wonders who she was with when she bought it. They kiss, on the cheek. In separate orbits they circle the table and sit. Perhaps the chairs are too close. The half-finished candle flickers. It has been a long time.

Pierre offers the wine. She smiles, takes a sip, rolls it across her tongue.

'It's perfect,' she says, not meaning anything at all.

Their conversation stumbles, an awkward duet. He talks about Oxford. She brings news of Paris. And after a while, when they have nothing left to say, they talk about the weather.

అంరుదాంశ్

*The Oxford Castle scheme includes a hotel in the Malmaison chain, Malmaison Oxford, occupying a large part of the former prison block, with converted jail cells as guest rooms. This is the first time in the UK that a prison has been turned into a hotel.*

# *Biographies*

As a former publisher, **Andrew Bax** spent much of his life issuing deadlines to busy professionals who had very little time for writing. Now he has started to write himself he wonders why none of them, as far as he knows, blew a gasket.

**Vicky Mancuso Brehm.** Born in Canada and raised in Brazil and Italy, Vicky Mancuso Brehm studied geography at Hertford College. She works as a researcher in international development, and lives near Oxford with her husband and two children.

**Janet Bolam** was brought up next to the ultimate playground - a farm complete with cows, chickens, geese, a pony and resident children. Now she plays with theatre, writing and grandchildren.

**Kathleen Daly** lives in Oxford with a rescue border collie, a retired Riding for the Disabled horse and a physicist husband.

**Ann Edwards** lives in a small village in Oxfordshire. She is married with three children, has a one eyed pug, a magnificent cat, a foul tempered parrot and four hens. She likes to talk about writing and has given up cooking for watching the telly.

**Wendy Greenberg** (plus her husband and son) are housekeepers to 2 cats with attitude. When not tending to their every need she regularly escapes to a world of fiction - reading, writing and Ambridge. She also loves (in no particular order) the West Wing, Veuve Cliquot, good food, the sea and singing in the car.

**Kamini Khanduri** lives in Oxford (where she was born) with her husband and two daughters. She works as an editor at a book publishing company. When she's not at work, she enjoys doing crosswords, eating in restaurants, talking to friends, going to the seaside, and watching Dr Who.

**Nichola May** home educates her three children and is in her final year of a Diploma in Creative Writing. She keeps chickens and a badly behaved spaniel.

**Jackie Vickers** keeps neither mad hens nor crazy pets. She does, however, care about the fate of badgers and this year's fledglings. Writing about animals can provide a welcome diversion from reality.

BOMBUS
BOOKS